Without Regret

By Nicole Edwards

The Alluring Indulgence Series

Kaleb
Zane
Travis
Holidays with the Walker Brothers
Ethan
Braydon
Sawyer
Brendon

The Austin Arrows Series

Rush
Kaufman

The Bad Boys of Sports Series

Bad Reputation
Bad Business

The Caine Cousins Series

Hard to Hold
Hard to Handle

The Club Destiny Series

Conviction
Temptation
Addicted
Seduction
Infatuation
Captivated
Devotion
Perception
Entrusted
Adored
Distraction

The Coyote Ridge Series

Curtis
Jared

The Dead Heat Ranch Series

Boots Optional
Betting on Grace
Overnight Love

By Nicole Edwards (cont.)

The Devil's Bend Series

Chasing Dreams
Vanishing Dreams

The Devil's Playground Series

Without Regret
Without Restraint

The Office Intrigue Series

Office Intrigue
Intrigued Out of the Office
Their Rebellious Submissive

The Pier 70 Series

Reckless
Fearless
Speechless
Harmless

The Sniper 1 Security Series

Wait for Morning
Never Say Never
Tomorrow's Too Late

The Southern Boy Mafia Series

Beautifully Brutal
Beautifully Loyal

Standalone Novels

A Million Tiny Pieces
Inked on Paper

Writing as Timberlyn Scott

Unhinged
Unraveling
Chaos

Naughty Holiday Editions

2015
2016

Without Regret

Devil's Playground
Book 1

NICOLE EDWARDS

Nicole Edwards Limited
PO Box 806
Hutto, Texas 78634
www.slipublishing.com
www.NicoleEdwardsLimited.com

Cover Image: © essl | 123rf.com (9613668)
Cover Design: © Nicole Edwards Limited
Editing: Blue Otter Editing www.BlueOtterEditing.com

ISBN (ebook): 978-1-939786-48-7
ISBN (print): 978-1-939786-47-0

1

THE DARK INTERIOR of the casino called his name, but Isaiah Fontenot doubted the voices were saying the same things to him that they were saying to most of the people surrounding him.

Hit me!

Stand!

Come on, six!

No, those weren't the same voices he was hearing. Not today, anyway.

Isaiah wasn't drawn to the flashing lights of the slot machines or the cheers coming from the blackjack tables. Nor did he find any interest in the chaos that surrounded the craps tables.

Then again, he wasn't a gambler—at least not when it came to casino games. Other things in life, sure.

So, it only made sense that he wasn't hearing *those* voices in his head as he snaked his way through the various slot machines, past the line of blackjack tables teeming with people. Unlike most of the people in the place, he wasn't seeking a way to discard some of his hard-earned money in minutes. No, Isaiah was actually looking for someone.

A woman.

More accurately, a beautiful woman. One who had found herself in a shit ton of trouble as of late and had somehow ended up as Isaiah's problem.

Being that he was from Las Vegas, lived and worked on the Vegas strip—in the very casino he currently traversed, in fact—Isaiah didn't have much interest in the tourist hot spot, didn't find intrigue in the sights and sounds of money being spent hand over fist in an effort to hit the big one, all with enormous hopes of coming out a winner. However, he did see the merits of using the place as a hideout, as the woman seemed to be doing.

With a cautious eye on his surroundings, Isaiah continued toward the bar.

Nope, nothing.

No spark of excitement in his gut, no antsy fingers ready to hit or stand. In fact, Isaiah was certain he'd been desensitized to it over the years. Although he wasn't opposed to gambling as a whole, he simply tended to lean toward a different type of risk, something a little less … controlled.

Not to mention, the family he worked for wouldn't take too kindly to him gambling on the job. He'd been sent on this particular mission to locate a specific person, who, according to his boss, wouldn't be too keen on going with him once he did finally locate her, but that was a challenge Isaiah was up for.

Good thing he knew how to make things happen. It was one of the reasons the family he worked for depended on him and his twin brother, Micah, to run the show in Las Vegas. They'd been in charge of one of Vegas's swankiest nightclubs, Devil's Playground, for the past five years and had, over time, established quite the reputation.

As he eased up against the bar, Isaiah peered around, pretending to be looking for someone. It was partially true, he *was* looking for someone, someone he'd already located. In fact, he'd made eye contact with the copper-haired goddess, even offered a smile that reflected his feigned interest. Or he hoped it had, anyway.

Perhaps this wouldn't be so bad after all.

In an attempt to appear casual, Isaiah ordered a drink and then retrieved his cell phone from his pocket while he waited. Thumbing the screen, he pulled up his contact list. He didn't have to scroll too far to find the information for Maximillian Adorite. Pulling the number up, he hit the button to send a text.

Found her.

Less than a minute later, he received a response: **Report when you have more information.**

Knowing his boss didn't need unnecessary pleasantries, Isaiah pocketed his phone as he retrieved his drink from the bartender. He sipped the top-shelf, single malt scotch, allowing his gaze to once again roam the area. His mark hadn't left from where she sat alone at a corner table. She looked nervous as hell, and Isaiah couldn't very well blame her. Despite the fact that he worked for the Texas family known as the Southern Boy Mafia, by far one of the most powerful and influential organized crime families in Texas, this girl … well, she'd inadvertently gotten in bed with some pretty nasty people, and his boss had asked that he pull her into the fold in order to protect her.

Strange, that. Isaiah wasn't used to tracking people, or saving them, as was the case here, but he didn't defy orders—nor did he question them—when they came down.

So here he was.

Waiting.

Max Adorite wasn't known much for his kindness, but ever since Max had married Courtney Kogan, he'd gotten a little soft. Not that Isaiah would ever let anyone hear him say that. After all, he didn't have a death wish. Apparently, with this particular gig, Max was doing a favor for his wife. According to the information he'd been given, the mystery woman's family had sought out the Sniper 1 Security team to help locate, and protect, the woman's brother, and since Courtney's family owned the business, and the incident was in Vegas, they'd leaned on her to help out because they knew Max had business there.

And now Isaiah was involved.

Micah should've been, as well, but … he was MIA. As was usually the case during the daylight hours.

For a brief moment, Isaiah allowed his gaze to slide over the mystery woman whose life he was about to save, although his methods would likely be questioned. Not that he gave a shit. He got things done, and he knew just what the situation warranted.

He'd known what she looked like thanks to the picture Max had provided, but the camera hadn't done her justice. Her long hair looked like copper silk hanging over her slender shoulders and caressing the tops of her breasts. From his vantage point, he could also tell that she had a really, *really* nice rack—something that hadn't been evident in her picture—hidden beneath a snug, black tank top.

Her clear, sea-green eyes glimmered in the dim lights shining over her as she peered out from beneath her lashes, pretending not to notice him watching her. With the way the lights shone down on her, her alabaster skin appeared soft and smooth, and despite his mission and the notion that the woman would likely freak once he officially introduced himself, Isaiah couldn't deny the instant attraction he felt for her.

Not that he was looking for a woman. He had enough of those to deal with on a nightly basis, all types, all races, all shapes and sizes. He loved women, all of them, but he didn't have to go searching for one. Being that he managed Devil's Playground—Max's Vegas nightclub, named the same as its sister locations in Dallas and New York—he had his pick of the litter on any given night. Since the club was located in one of the ritziest hotels on the strip, Isaiah didn't have to worry about relationships, either, thanks to the tourists who strolled in and out of his world almost instantly. In this city, people were usually just visiting, merely a temporary distraction, as far as he was concerned.

But tonight, before he went to work, Isaiah had another job. One that required him to move away from the bar and talk to this woman before she slipped away and he had to spend hours searching for her again.

When she finished her drink, he decided to make his move. Taking his glass with him, he made his way over to her. Smiling, he decided to forego a cheesy line in the hopes that direct would be the better angle.

"Mind if I buy you a drink?" he asked as he approached, watching the attractive woman intently.

And for the first time in all of his thirty-eight years, Isaiah experienced something he'd never encountered before. The woman whose attention he was looking to attract took one look at him and ... panicked.

Yep, that was certainly new.

2

LORD. HAVE. MERCY.

Any other day, any other place … Cassidy Owens could've been tempted by the handsome stranger who approached her so casually.

Not today.

Nuh-uh.

Sure, she had noticed the tall, well-dressed, dark-haired man sitting at the bar, eyeing her as though he had a craving for something sweet and she'd been dipped in sugar. He was one of those men who drew attention without even trying, and she'd been almost flattered by the fact that he'd turned all that heat on her as soon as he'd glanced her way. Tall, with broad shoulders and nicely styled short hair … he was attractive in a way that screamed wealth and power.

At first, she'd paid him no mind, or pretended to, anyway. Aside from admiring him briefly, she'd done her best not to look his way. However, since then, she'd been well aware that he was watching her. And now that he approached, her internal alarm system was shrieking loudly, leaving her with only one choice.

Flee.

Logical, right?

As she pushed back from the table, the chair she'd been seated in toppled to the ground, and she used the distraction to make her escape.

"Going somewhere, sweetheart?"

Oh, hell.

Doing a double take, Cassidy's head snapped around on her neck as she looked from one man to the other.

Uhh … there were two of them.

Two.

How was that even possible?

One would've been enough, but two… That was far too much temptation.

Unfortunately, she didn't have time to get the answer to that question because her fight-or-flight instinct had kicked in, and she knew she had to go. Far and fast.

With a quick, dismissive smile, she found an opening and took it, stepping down from the tiered floor of the bar and onto the casino floor, ducking slightly so that she'd blend in with the group of people crowding around the craps table.

Okay, so she wasn't incredibly naïve. Cassidy knew that the handsome duo hadn't just been hitting on her, nor were they sitting back and wondering why the hell she'd run when offered a drink. Nope, she'd seen that knowing gleam in the first guy's eyes. Their brief introduction hadn't been happenstance, which was why she was still hauling ass as fast as her three-inch wedge heels would take her. She doubted she could outrun them, but Cassidy had something spurring her on—a very strong, very determined will to live.

Using the overly crowded casino to her advantage, she maneuvered through the packed place, slipping between one set of slot machines, then another, getting lost in the groups of people crowded around, until she wound up in the high rollers lounge, the inquisitive attendants' eyes instantly seeking her out.

Crap.

Not exactly where she had intended to go, but as she glanced around, it looked as though she'd accomplished her goal. The dark-haired strangers were nowhere to be found, thank goodness.

"Shit," she said on a long exhale.

"Can I get you something?" a young blonde woman with a bored expression asked as she made a quick pass by, holding a tray and a tablet at the ready.

"No, thanks," Cassidy answered softly, turning her attention to another machine, faking interest. When the waitress disappeared, Cassidy allowed several minutes to pass while she pretended to peruse the various machines that required a fifteen-dollar minimum bet. *Minimum*! Holy crap. Like she would ever waste that kind of money.

But that was honestly the last thing on her mind.

Peering out of the room through the clouded-glass windows, watching the people milling about, she didn't see her pursuers.

Had it really been that easy? Slipping away from those two?

One could only hope, but Cassidy doubted that the men who were after her would be so easy to evade. After all, if they were the ones who'd trashed her condo … well, Cassidy knew the night was far from over.

Taking a deep breath, she scanned the area outside of the room and decided the coast was clear. As clear as it was going to get, anyhow.

She needed to get somewhere less public, preferably a place no one would think to look for her. Granted, she didn't know where else to go since she'd spent the last two days at the hotel, sleeping when she could—which consisted of approximately three fitful hours in a forty-eight-hour period—and trying to get in touch with her brother. Unfortunately, she'd had to use her credit card for the room, and likely that had sent up red flags, which had brought those men after her.

If only she could talk to her brother. Jordan would know what to do, but for whatever reason, he wasn't answering, and that was what had her most worried.

So, sure, she was sleep deprived, a little irritable, but she wasn't dumb. Paranoid, maybe. Dumb, no.

Sliding into a group of people, Cassidy followed them toward the hotel lobby. If she could only reach the elevator without being seen by the dynamic duo, she'd be home free.

Several tense minutes later, with a sigh of relief, Cassidy punched the button that would call the elevator while she watched several people standing around, animatedly talking about their plans for the evening. The bell dinged, signaling the arrival of the car. The instant the doors opened, Cassidy sidestepped the people exiting so they wouldn't run her down, and then she slipped into the elevator behind them. A chorus of greetings sounded in the narrow corridor, which must've meant the people who'd come down had joined their party. As the doors began to close, she realized she was alone in the car.

Thank goodn—

Shit.

Her relief was short-lived when a large hand interrupted the doors from closing.

Oh, hell.

"Relax," the dark-haired man from the bar said as he joined her inside the car, his duplicate following close behind him.

Cassidy was tempted to scream, but her shock halted the sound in her throat as she stared at the intimidating men eyeing her closely. Then the doors closed, sealing the three of them inside. Alone.

Yep, she was going to die, no doubt about it. And to think, she'd been waiting until next month—when she turned thirty—to start checking off things on her bucket list.

That's what you get for procrastinating, Cass.

"We're not here to hurt you," one of them explained, his voice gruff. "Hit the button for your floor."

"Like hell," she replied, grateful her voice was strong and steady now.

Not dumb, remember?

"You've got two options, Cassidy. We either get to your hotel room, get your shit, and get you to safety, or we head to the top floor, where we can at least protect you."

"Protect me?" she asked, the incredulity evident in her tone. He couldn't think she was that gullible, could he? "Protect me from who? You?"

The second man spoke, his voice sounding eerily the same as the other guy's. "In a second, someone is going to hit the call button, and the doors'll open again. The next person to get in the elevator might not have your best interests in mind."

Cassidy snorted her disbelief. "Are you—?"

"Questions later," the first man scolded while the other one hit the button for the top floor.

Her eyes widened as she realized what was happening. They were kidnapping her and they… "Wait. How do you know my name?"

Oh, God. It was true. The bad guys had found her.

Neither man said anything, glancing at one another before turning to face the elevator doors.

They were both immaculately dressed in what she could only assume were expensive suits. Despite the fact that they were big and broad, Cassidy noticed something else about them both. They were packing. And she wasn't referring to the mountains of muscles beneath those suits. She'd seen enough movies to know that those were guns pressing against their jackets, and her mouth suddenly went dry.

"Where are you taking me?" she finally asked as the elevator continued to rise, passing one floor after another.

While she waited for an answer, she tried to come up with an escape plan. Throughout her life, she'd never learned what to do in a situation such as this. Even her master's degree in sociology hadn't helped her—nor did her administrative job in the health care system—despite the fact that she could practically predict what would happen next. Human behavior and all that.

Knowing there were some very dangerous men looking for her—all in an effort to get their hands on her brother—Cassidy hadn't planned ahead for the point when they would finally catch up to her. In fact, she'd hoped to never get to that point.

Too late now.

"The least you can do is tell me who you are before you kill me."

Both men peered over their shoulders at her, matching smirks lifting the corners of their lips.

"Name's Isaiah," the one on the right said easily. "Isaiah Fontenot. This is my brother, Micah."

Well, that was a start. It meant little to her, but at least they'd gotten past the ignoring her part.

Feeling lucky, she decided to go for broke. "What do you want from me?"

"*From* you?"

The guy on the right—Isaiah—continued to glance back at her, his grin wicked, but for some reason, Cassidy didn't fear him. Not entirely, anyway. Why, she had no idea.

"We're doing a favor for our boss," Isaiah explained. "And no, before you freak out again, we're not planning to kill you. You'll get all your questions answered when we get to the room. You can call him."

"Who's your boss?" she asked, but the doors opened before he had a chance to answer.

Cassidy found herself being ushered out of the elevator, down a long hallway, then through another set of doors, another hallway, and finally another elevator. Once inside, Micah hit the button for the top floor, which, in that particular elevator, was different from the last one.

If she hadn't been nervous before, she was now.

Less than a minute later, the elevator came to a stop, and she was once again ushered out.

With shaking hands, she gripped her purse, wishing like hell she'd thought to grab her trusty can of mace before she'd hightailed it out of her condo. Hindsight.

Isaiah—she could only tell them apart thanks to the different colors of their suits—ran a key card through the electronic reader on the door they came to, and the lock disengaged. While Micah remained behind her, Isaiah led the way into the room.

For some stupid reason, Cassidy dutifully followed. And now the jury was officially out on the not-dumb claim she'd made earlier.

"Evening," a stocky blond man said by way of greeting. "Everything's cool here. I'll wait in the hall."

With that, the guy was gone.

"Who was that?"

"Security."

Who the hell were these people?

Unable to voice her question or to get her feet to carry her forward, Cassidy didn't budge until Micah urged her forward.

"We're not the good guys, Cassidy, but I assure you we're better than the ones after you."

Well, since he put it that way… What the hell was that supposed to mean?

Before she could put sound to the words bouncing on her tongue, she was pushed inside the room, and the door was closed and locked behind them. Instinct kicked in, and Cassidy searched the room for a weapon, anything that she could use to fend these men off, because no matter what they told her, she believed, without a doubt, that they were *not* the good guys. After all, they both had a dark, mysterious edge that made her keenly aware of them. If she had to guess, they were the type of men people didn't fuck with.

The only question left was … how bad were they?

3

ISAIAH KNEW THE moment they stepped inside his penthouse that things were about to go to hell if he didn't think of something fast. Mainly due to the fact Cassidy Owens was seeking a weapon, her distrust in them apparent. But also because he could sense something in his brother that wasn't quite copacetic. He appeared irritated.

"We're not gonna hurt you," Micah grumbled, walking away from Cassidy when she didn't seem interested in going any farther into the room.

Isaiah watched as her gaze strayed to the door.

"Frank's outside," he told her. "You won't make it far, so just relax."

Not that he expected her to do as he said, but it was worth a shot.

He had to give his boss credit, Max sure knew how to pick them. From the instant Isaiah had laid eyes on the redhead, he'd been battling a case of insta-lust. Some serious shit, at that. What it was about her, he wasn't entirely sure, either, but if he had to guess, this deep-rooted desire wasn't going to go away, even if the girl did.

Woman.

Not girl.

From what he knew of Cassidy Owens, she was a healthy, smart twenty-nine-year-old woman who lived and worked close by, had all of her life. Aside from her brother—who apparently had a gambling problem—she had a set of parents who'd moved to Florida a few years back. She worked at one of the local hospitals in a human services job that she'd held since she'd graduated from college eight years earlier.

Smart, reliable. Beautiful.

Oh, and she was running from some really nasty guys.

Then again, his attraction to her wasn't unheard of. It wasn't as though he didn't meet attractive women on a nightly basis. Running a Vegas nightclub with his brother pretty well guaranteed him sex. Especially when women found out who they really were. The fact that they managed a nightclub like Devil's Playground tended to impress a lot of people.

Isaiah got the sense that Cassidy wouldn't be all that impressed.

Which probably explained why he was rather anxious to show the sexy little woman currently trying to find a way out of the penthouse just what he was capable of, how easily he could make her body burn for him.

Not that he intended to offer as much. At least not yet.

"So what now?" Cassidy asked, still standing in the foyer clutching her purse to her chest.

"First, we move this little party farther inside. Then, we'll call Max."

"Who's Max?"

"Max Adorite. Our boss."

Her eyes widened, and Isaiah figured that meant she'd heard of him. Considering Max's name was often tossed around, it wasn't unheard of. The Adorites had established quite the name for themselves in the gaming and hotel industry over the last few years.

Without waiting for her to follow, Isaiah decided to venture toward his office, wanting to get this show on the road. As he made his way through the dining room, where Micah was currently waiting, then farther down the hall, he heard his brother's footsteps behind him.

Less than a minute later, Isaiah was sitting at his desk, his cell phone in hand.

He looked up, his eyebrows lifting in a silent question when Micah entered the room behind him. Alone.

"She's coming," Micah reassured him, obviously reading Isaiah's mind. "Go ahead and call Max. I've got things to do."

When Cassidy joined them a moment later, Micah directed her toward one of the chairs opposite Isaiah's desk. After she reluctantly took a seat, Micah followed suit, lowering himself into the chair beside her while Isaiah kept an eye on her.

Isaiah placed his phone on the desk, the speaker engaged, the annoying ring filling the silence.

"Where is she?" Max inquired without a hello.

"Here with me," Isaiah informed him. "We're at the penthouse."

"Good," Max grumbled. "She's safe then?"

Isaiah smiled but didn't look at Cassidy. She was definitely safe. From danger, anyway. As for how safe she was from him … well, that was a different story.

Isaiah leaned forward, his forearms resting on his desk as he shed the smile and cast a glance at Cassidy.

While Max rambled, Isaiah did his best to pay attention, but his thoughts had drifted in a different direction, one that involved the sweet Cassidy Owens naked. Perhaps draped across his desk while Isaiah fed her his cock.

Mmm. Hell yes.

Micah spoke up, drawing Isaiah to the present.

He had no idea what they were talking about but figured he should probably pay attention. Whatever his boss had to say was meant more for Cassidy than for him. Saving women from imminent death wasn't Isaiah's forte—and before today, he hadn't thought it to be something he'd be attempting anytime in his future. He had no idea what they were supposed to do with her at this point (though he had a few suggestions), and in just a couple of hours, when Devil's Playground opened its doors for the night, his entire focus would be on the club and not on the girl.

"Cassidy, my name's Max Adorite. My wife and I are here to help you."

Cassidy's wide green eyes centered on Isaiah's face as though she was seeking his input. Regarding what, Isaiah didn't know. It'd been a long time since he'd circled a woman rather than getting right to the point. Unlike this situation with Cassidy, when it came to the other women he chose to spend his time with, his intentions were usually sexual in nature. Those he met at the club usually knew the score before he ever got them naked, but Isaiah knew that wouldn't work well with Cassidy.

However, he certainly wondered what would.

Shaking off the thought, Isaiah knew he needed to keep this on a more professional level. While Max continued to talk to Cassidy, Isaiah got up and nodded for his twin to join him in the hall.

"What do we do with her now?" Micah inquired as soon as they were out of earshot of the phone.

Isaiah's eyes traveled past Micah and back into the room where Cassidy was. "No idea."

"She looks exhausted," Micah said. "Maybe she can sleep while we go to work."

"Not sure she'll trust us enough to sleep here."

"Then get her her own suite. I'm sure she'd be open to that."

Isaiah shook his head. "She's safer with us."

For now.

Isaiah leaned one shoulder against the doorjamb, watching Cassidy. The first thing he noticed was that her eyes had softened somewhat, the lines bracketing her mouth not quite so harsh, and her shoulders were a little less tense. Obviously her conversation with Max had put her at ease. And that was a good thing.

"What does Max want us to do?" Micah inquired from behind him.

"For now, keep her out of sight while we track down her brother."

As Isaiah watched Cassidy's gaze search the room, he figured that was easier said than done. At the same time, he wondered whether or not she would come to trust them, hoping until that time came she would do as instructed. It wasn't in her best interest to ignore Max. As it was, she was in deep shit, and it would only get worse if she didn't allow someone to help her.

"Cassidy," Max said sternly, his gruff tone echoing in the office, "I want you to talk to my wife, Courtney. She's gonna ask you some questions. Be as honest as you can be, understood?"

"Yes, I understand," Cassidy agreed reluctantly, still talking to Max.

A second later, Courtney Adorite's voice sounded on the other end of the line. Isaiah continued to listen from the doorway while Max's wife questioned Cassidy about her brother's whereabouts. Cassidy wasn't a fountain of information, but she was cooperative.

While he listened, he tried to figure out what the hell he was supposed to do with the woman. Micah was right, she looked as though she were going to fall over at any moment. He hadn't noticed earlier, but there were dark circles beneath her eyes. Probably from lack of sleep. According to what Max had told him initially, Cassidy Owens was on the run and had been for a couple of days since someone had trashed her condo in an effort to locate her brother, Jordan.

And while Cassidy explained her situation to Max's wife, Isaiah had to wonder just what the hell he had gotten himself into.

But more importantly, how he was to get them all out of this.

Alive.

4

CASSIDY WAS EXHAUSTED, but she wasn't sure she'd ever be able to sleep again.

After practically telling her life's story to the man on the phone, and then retelling it and more to the woman, blindly trusting this Courtney Adorite to get her out of this mess, she'd kept her eye on Isaiah, right up to the point he'd come back to the desk and ended the call, placing his cell phone back into his pocket.

Despite the danger that seemed to be her life at the moment, Cassidy found herself strangely drawn to the man who'd come to her rescue.

What was it they called that? When the hostage had positive feelings toward her captor?

Stockholm syndrome.

Yes, that was it. Maybe she had that.

After all, Cassidy knew nothing about him, other than he'd said he wouldn't kill her, but at the same time, how did she know he was telling the truth? Maybe they weren't the men after her, but they didn't look like white knights ready to whisk her away to safety, either. There was no doubt in her mind that she would be tortured if the guys who were after her brother got their hands on her. According to Courtney, they were after her brother because he'd gone bad on a loan.

Cassidy had already known that much. Her brother… Well, Jordan had problems, problems no one could fix until he was ready to help himself.

And look where his problems had landed her.

As much as Cassidy wanted to acknowledge that this was her reality, she had a hard time believing it all. This was mobster-type stuff. And yes, having grown up in Vegas, she knew all about the mob. After all, they were credited with laying the groundwork that had become Sin City.

"You okay? Need anything?" Isaiah's deep voice broke into her thoughts, pulling her to the present.

"A nap," she retorted snidely.

"That can be arranged," he told her.

Cassidy's eyes lifted to meet Isaiah's shimmering mocha-brown gaze. "I hope that's not a double entendre."

Isaiah laughed, and the sound hit a nerve deep in her core. He was sexy as hell, although she knew that should've been the last thing on her mind at the moment.

"This is my private residence, so you can stay here. The club'll open in about an hour, so I have to go to work, but you'll be safe here."

"Will I?" Cassidy wasn't sure she'd be safe anywhere ever again. Not until they found Jordan, and she only prayed that Courtney managed to find him first. Then, perhaps he wouldn't die. After all, although Courtney had promised they'd keep her safe, the overly confident woman had never guaranteed Jordan's safety.

"Come on," Isaiah said softly, reaching for her hand and helping her from her chair.

With her hand in his, Cassidy suddenly felt way too underdressed. The tank top and shorts she'd thought were a good idea that morning left her chilled in the air-conditioned room. However, she wasn't sure she'd ever be warm again, either. Not until they found Jordan and she knew he was safe.

That was what it all came down to at this point. Her brother. His safety.

God, she was tired.

"I'm heading out," Micah said from the doorway, his gaze traveling over them both briefly.

Cassidy studied him for a moment. Although there was no doubt he was Isaiah's twin, the more she looked at him, the less like his brother he appeared. His dark hair was a little longer, his brown eyes a little less intense. He was the fun-loving one, she figured.

"I'll talk to you later at the club," Micah told Isaiah before slipping down the hall and out of sight.

Cassidy glanced up at Isaiah once again.

"Come on. I'll show you around. Then I've got to get downstairs."

Once Isaiah left her in his penthouse a good half hour later, Cassidy could hardly keep her eyes open. He'd given her a T-shirt and shorts to change into in the event she wanted to take a shower, and she was debating what to do next.

It didn't appear as though he was keeping her there against her will. In fact, she was almost certain she could waltz right out of that room and then right out of the hotel if she wanted to.

But she didn't want to.

Glancing over at the huge king-sized bed with the plain black comforter and large fluffy pillows, she felt her eyelids grow heavier. Maybe she could sleep for a little while, and then, when morning came, she'd be able to think more clearly.

First a shower.

After disrobing and delicately placing her discarded clothes in a pile on the counter, Cassidy scanned the room. The décor was modern, and the feel was overtly masculine. On one of the sinks sat a can of shaving cream, a razor, toothpaste, and a toothbrush. All neatly arranged.

The towels were folded as though the housekeeping service for the hotel also serviced Isaiah's penthouse, which she figured was the case. It explained the pristine counters and floors.

After taking the rug from its perch over a towel bar on the shower door, Cassidy set two white towels on a ledge nearby and climbed into the shower.

While she allowed the warm water to rain down on her in the massive glass stall, Cassidy thought back to her last conversation with her brother. He'd been scared, telling her she needed to leave town for a little while. He had suggested she go visit their parents in Florida, but Cassidy had refused. She had a job, after all. A job that probably wasn't there for her anymore now that she hadn't shown up or called in two days. Did they wonder what had happened to her? Or had they gone as business as usual without her there?

Sighing heavily, Cassidy reached for the shampoo.

Fifteen minutes later, she forced her weary body out of the shower. After winding her hair into one of the towels and drying off with the other, she pulled on the clothes Isaiah had loaned her. They hung on her, but they weren't too bad. Better than putting on what she'd been wearing.

Crawling into bed, she tried her best to ignore the scent of the man that washed over her. It was a sexy, seductive smell that made her body ache for some comfort. From Isaiah.

"You're going crazy," she said aloud after closing her eyes.

And that was the last thing she remembered before drifting off into blessed sleep.

5

"HEY, BOSS," VAN greeted when Isaiah stepped up to the bar to check on his main bartender. "Guy was over here asking about you a few minutes ago."

Isaiah nodded.

He knew that Van wasn't talking about just any customer. He wouldn't have bothered to share that information if it wasn't important.

"Said he'll find you later."

Great. Just fucking perfect. He doubted this man was looking for him, but rather, was looking for Cassidy Owens.

By now, the word was probably out that Max Adorite had intervened and was keeping Cassidy within his protection. Since this was Vegas and Isaiah and Micah were known to handle Max's business dealings in Sin City, it made sense that the guy was seeking Isaiah out.

Figuring shit was going to go down regardless, Isaiah shot a quick text to Max, letting him know that the guys looking for Cassidy had come to the club. He'd wait to see how Max wanted to handle things before he made any moves.

Isaiah managed Devil's Playground, but that wasn't the extent of his job duties. After all, when he'd signed on with the Adorite family years ago, he hadn't been disillusioned about what they did or who they were. And it didn't matter what they asked of him, Isaiah was loyal to the Adorites. Always would be.

The life he lived wasn't simple, nor was it easy. Never had been. Having grown up in a town known for its debauchery and poverty, Isaiah had done what needed to be done in order for him and Micah to survive. After his parents had been murdered when he and Micah were nineteen, he'd dedicated his life to surviving. Which was how, years later, he'd ended up with the Adorites. The only family he and Micah had. They watched his back and he watched theirs.

Now, he had to make sure he protected Cassidy Owens at all costs because that was what Max had asked of him.

"I'm heading up. Call me if you need anything. Tony's at the door. Have you seen Micah?" Isaiah had only seen his twin brother briefly since he'd come down to the club. They'd talked about a couple of issues, but then Micah had gone off on his own to handle something.

"He's around here somewhere. Saw him earlier," Van informed him as he prepared a drink, grinning and winking at some chick who was eyeing him from the other side of the bar.

"If you see him, tell him I went up. He can handle closing."

"Will do, boss."

With that, Isaiah left the club and ventured up to his penthouse. Doing his best to keep quiet, he slipped inside, nodding to Frank, who was still standing guard outside the penthouse door.

After pulling off his jacket and laying it over the arm of a dining room chair, Isaiah loosened his tie and headed down the narrow hall to the bedroom. He found Cassidy asleep in his bed, tangled up in the black silk sheets, her fiery hair haphazardly strewn across his pillow.

Unable to help himself, Isaiah admired her in the light from the bathroom that spilled into the room. She wasn't the sweet angel he'd imagined her to be when she was asleep, and that pulled a smile from him. The woman hogged the entire bed, limbs flung about, her mouth slightly open, her breaths deep and even.

She looked like a woman who hadn't slept in a decade, and yet she was still the most beautiful woman he'd seen in a long damn time.

What was it about her that intrigued him so much? He couldn't answer that question because he knew so little about her. In fact, he didn't know a damn thing about her other than her basic history and that there were some crazy fucks out to get her brother and they weren't above using her to get to him.

"What time is it?"

Isaiah smiled into the darkness, watching as Cassidy rolled over and hugged the pillow.

"Almost four," he told her.

"In the morning?"

"Yeah. Go back to sleep."

"Where will you sleep?" she mumbled.

He wouldn't, but he didn't tell her as much. "The couch."

When her deep breathing resumed, Isaiah slipped out of the bedroom and back to the living room, then over to the small kitchenette. He headed to the refrigerator, grabbed a bottle of water, and then slipped into his office, leaving the door open so he could hear Cassidy if she needed him.

Pulling open his laptop, he started doing his own research, checking into the things Max had sent him via email. By the time the sun broke over the mountains, he'd learned a hell of a lot more about Cassidy Owens, but not enough that he could figure out a way to get her out of the situation she found herself in.

Truth was, if they were going to get to the bottom of this, they were going to have to put their boots to the ground. More than likely, they were going to have to draw these bastards out.

And he had a pretty good idea of just how to do that.

6

CASSIDY ROLLED OVER and, through blurry eyes, scanned the nightstand for the clock. When she saw the time, she fell onto her back and sighed. She'd slept for six hours, which was twice as long as she'd slept in the last couple of days. Oddly enough, she felt better than she had since she'd fled her trashed condo earlier in the week, but like every day, the first thought that came to mind was her brother.

Was Jordan alive? Had he purposely abandoned her knowing she would have to settle his debt? *Could* she settle his debt?

At this point, she didn't know exactly how much he owed—somewhere between twenty and forty thousand according to her brother—but Courtney Adorite had promised to find that out for her. After Courtney had explained that Cassidy's parents had contacted Sniper 1 Security to help her out of this mess, her mind had been somewhat put at ease. Except for the part that was still worried about Jordan.

The only positive was that she had someone helping her.

Her mind drifted to Isaiah and his twin brother, Micah. Closing her eyes, she remembered seeing them both for the first time. Perhaps her fear had made them appear larger than life, Isaiah even more so than Micah. There was something strangely erotic about the man. He made her think of hot, dirty sex, and that image was exactly what her mind conjured—as well as her dreams—as she lay in his bed. She could still smell him, a heady, masculine scent that made her feel oddly safe.

She wished he were there with her, if only to put the last of her fears to rest. She could practically imagine what it would feel like to be wrapped in his arms, held against his hard body.

And no, she wasn't the type of girl who could go to bed with a man on the first night she met him. Never pretended to be. Her life had been spent on the straight and narrow. She didn't get into trouble, didn't date the bad boy because he made her heart rate spike. She tended to lean toward safe men. Didn't mean she couldn't fantasize, though. At the moment, it was the only thing she could do in order to not think about the danger that had closed ranks around her life and seemingly put her in a choke hold.

"We need to run an errand."

Cassidy's eyes flew open, and she saw Isaiah standing above her. She knew it was him based on the intent glimmer in his dark eyes. Unlike his brother, Isaiah didn't have laugh lines around his eyes. From the very first moment she'd seen him, he'd been nothing but serious. And grumpy.

Well, except for that wicked smirk he'd shot her in the elevator. But that didn't count.

"Where?" she questioned, forcing herself to sit up and drop her legs over the side of the bed.

"Your condo."

"What?" Her eyes widened as she took in his more-than-serious expression. "Why?"

"To get some of your things. And then we need to swing by your brother's place. See if we can find anything helpful."

"My brother … uh…" *How did she put this?* "He doesn't have a place."

One of Isaiah's dark eyebrows lifted slightly.

"He sorta stays with me when he needs somewhere to go."

"Then we'll search your place."

Cassidy wasn't sure that would do much good, but staying in bed all day sure wasn't going to get her anywhere, either.

Meeting his gaze, she nodded. "Give me a few minutes to get dressed."

As Isaiah walked out of the room, Cassidy pretended not to be worried about how the day would go. She also pretended not to stare at that man's extremely fine ass encased in those faded jeans.

Sadly, the first was easier to ignore than the second.

7

MICAH WAS SITTING in the car at the VIP entrance to the hotel, waiting for Isaiah and Cassidy when they came downstairs. From the looks of him, he hadn't been to bed yet, but that wasn't unusual for either of them. Isaiah hadn't bothered to sleep, either. When the club closed, he tended to be riding a wave of adrenaline for a few hours, which meant sleep didn't usually come until mid-morning. Looked like that would be delayed even longer today.

When Isaiah had contacted his brother to let him know they were heading to Cassidy's to check out her place, Micah hadn't sounded all that keen on the idea, but Isaiah knew his brother would do what needed to be done. He wasn't the type to shirk his responsibilities, no matter how much of a playboy he was.

And Micah was a playboy. Even more so than Isaiah. Not once in the last two decades since their parents had died had Micah ever had a serious relationship. At least not one that Isaiah knew about.

"Morning," Micah greeted them when they joined him in the car.

Isaiah helped Cassidy into the backseat before climbing into the passenger seat.

"Would it be possible to get something to eat?" Cassidy asked, her voice low as though she was scared to ask the question.

Micah glared over at Isaiah. "You didn't bother to feed the girl?"

Isaiah glared at him right back. Food had been the last thing on his mind.

"I know a place," Micah said, not waiting for Isaiah to give his approval, which was fine with him. The girl had to eat.

Fifteen minutes later, Micah parked the car in a small lot behind one of their favorite diners. It was a well-kept secret, off the strip and not privy to most of the tourists. Considering most visitors to Vegas didn't venture off the strip, it was one of those places the locals tended to frequent.

Once they were seated, with a round of coffee and three of the house specials ordered, the three of them sat quietly. Isaiah could've easily adapted to the silence for the next hour, but clearly Cassidy had other ideas.

"What are you hoping to find at my place?" Cassidy asked, peering between the two of them with acute interest.

Micah looked at Isaiah, giving him the opportunity to answer. He wasn't quite sure what they were hoping to find, other than perhaps a glimpse into the woman's life. Maybe something her brother had left behind that might lead them to his whereabouts. "Anything that'll lead us to where your brother might be."

"Do you think he's alive?" Cassidy asked, a note of sadness in her tone.

"Yes," Isaiah replied firmly. He had no reason to believe otherwise. "If he weren't, they wouldn't be after you."

"Why not?" she rebuked. "Wouldn't they still want their money?"

"Possibly," Isaiah replied. "But it usually doesn't work like that. Your brother's on the hook for the debt, not you. They'll settle the score with him any way they have to, even if it means hurting you to draw him out, or even by setting an example with him."

"By killing him, you mean?" Cassidy asked.

Isaiah nodded. That was exactly what he meant.

The waitress delivered their coffee and scurried off to the other side of the restaurant.

"Since they already trashed the place, don't you think they'd have found what they were looking for?" Cassidy's eyes slid over to Isaiah.

"Not necessarily."

"Did you call the cops?" Micah asked when Isaiah didn't elaborate.

"No," she said simply. "I'm a lot of things, but stupid isn't one of them."

Isaiah smiled as he stared down at his coffee. He liked the girl's gumption. She was smart and cautious, perhaps a tad fearless. A sexy combination.

"So what, specifically, will we be looking for?" she asked as they waited for their food.

"Anything to help us locate him."

"Why do you want to find him?" Cassidy inquired hesitantly, tearing open two packets of sugar and pouring them into her cup.

"So we can clear your name. It's the only way to keep you safe."

"What will you do to him when you find him?"

That was the million-dollar question. Isaiah had no idea what Max intended to do once they found Jordan Owens; he simply knew he was supposed to be looking for him. Were they going to hand him back over to these guys so he could take care of his debt? Doubtful. More than likely, Max would draw Jordan into the fold, if the man seemed worthy enough.

"Do you know where he might've gone?" Isaiah asked, ignoring Cassidy's question altogether.

"No," she answered, glancing down at the white ceramic mug in her hands. "I've tried to call him, but he's not answering."

"I doubt he kept his phone," Micah offered. "It'd be an easy way for them to track him down."

"Do you have family around here?" Isaiah asked, wondering if there was someone else these men might go after in order to get their hands on Jordan. With her parents in Florida, that was a little out of their way, but if she had, say, a grandmother or something, they'd need to devise another plan to keep her safe as well.

"No. My parents are in Florida, and they haven't seen him, either. Since he told me to go there before he ran, I doubt he'd go there. They'd find him."

Isaiah agreed. Jordan might have made some pretty powerful enemies, but at least he seemed to have his family's best interests at heart. Didn't help that he'd fled and now the guys he owed were coming after his sister, though.

"Any other family? Grandparents? Aunt? Uncle?"

"No," she said without blinking.

"What if we don't find him?" Cassidy asked, her clear green eyes sliding back and forth between the two of them.

"Let's not think about that just yet," Isaiah said. "Let's eat and we'll go from there."

Thankfully, the waitress delivered their food at that moment. Despite the millions of questions Isaiah had for the pretty redhead still staring at her coffee mug, he figured now wasn't the time to get into them.

If he was lucky—and he usually was—there'd be plenty of time for that later.

CASSIDY KNEW THAT she should've taken advantage of the silence when Isaiah all but instructed her to eat, but she was too nervous.

She blamed it on her curiosity.

Despite the strange fact that she trusted these men—although she knew nothing about them—she was still curious as to who they were, what they did. Why they would help her.

"What's on your mind?" Micah inquired as the two men dug into their food while Cassidy continued to play with her fork.

She shook her head, suddenly not wanting to voice her questions.

"Might as well spit it out," Isaiah grumbled.

Cassidy met his unyielding gaze. "Why are you helping me?"

"It's my job," he answered easily, never taking his eyes off her.

"I thought you worked at a club."

Isaiah smiled, and that small gesture sent a shiver of awareness through Cassidy. That minute gesture changed his appearance in ways she hadn't expected. He went from handsome to striking in an instant.

"We do. But that's not all we're capable of," he explained.

"Meaning you work for the mob?"

"Something like that," Micah added, not bothering to look up at her when he spoke.

"Is that who Max Adorite is? The mob?"

Isaiah set his fork down and picked up his coffee. "Max Adorite is a businessman. He's merely looking out for his interests."

Cassidy knew it was more than that. She'd gathered as much from their phone conversation last night. "How is helping me good for business?"

"It's not," Micah grumbled, and Cassidy got the sense that he wasn't all that fond of helping her.

Luckily, he wasn't the one in charge. At least from what she could tell.

"His wife asked him to," Isaiah told her.

She already knew that much.

Isaiah nodded toward her food and then said, "Eat. We've got things to do."

Cassidy did as he requested, barely tasting the eggs and bacon. Had it not been for the fact her stomach was grumbling from not eating in over twenty-four hours, she would've opted to forego food altogether. Then again, she wasn't sure when she'd get the chance to eat again. Not to mention, it had been her idea.

But in her defense, she'd merely been stalling, trying to get a better handle on who these two men were. Leading them to her condo, directly into her life, had been something she'd dreaded since the minute Isaiah had mentioned it.

Clearly she wasn't the one calling the shots, either.

"You talk to Max this morning?" Micah asked Isaiah.

Cassidy forced food into her mouth while she absently listened to them.

"Yeah. He asked about the man who sought me out at the club last night," Isaiah told him.

Micah's gaze lifted to meet Isaiah's directly, and Cassidy watched the interaction. There was a silent conversation that took place after that.

"Who?" she asked when Isaiah clearly didn't plan to go into detail.

"Don't know," he replied with a shrug, his gaze traveling over to her. "He never found me."

She didn't like the sound of that, but she kept that to herself. Once again turning her attention to her food, Cassidy fought the uneasiness that churned in her gut. For some reason, going to her condo didn't seem like the best plan, but considering Jordan still wasn't answering her calls, she didn't figure she had much of a choice.

It was that or run. And no matter how nervous she was, the last thing Cassidy wanted to do was run.

For some reason, she got the distinct impression she'd never be able to stop if she did.

And that was the last thing she wanted.

At least until she was completely out of options.

9

AFTER AN UNEVENTFUL breakfast where Cassidy remained remarkably quiet and Micah continued to eye her in a way that both intrigued Isaiah and brought out his possessive side, the three of them left the restaurant and headed straight for Cassidy's condo.

It didn't take long for them to get there, but from that point onward, the morning took a crazy shift and not in their favor.

"Let me have your key," Isaiah demanded when they arrived at her door on the eighth floor of the upscale building.

Truth was, Isaiah was a little surprised to see that Cassidy lived relatively close to the strip in a high-rise building that had a rather impressive view. Not that he'd known what to expect, because again, he knew very little about the woman.

"When was the last time you were here?" Micah asked, his voice low as he kept Cassidy close to him while Isaiah unlocked the door.

"Tuesday," she answered, her attention on the door. "I came home to find it trashed and didn't bother sticking around."

Smart girl.

Not knowing what to expect, Isaiah retrieved his gun from his shoulder holster and moved slowly inside, Cassidy and Micah following close behind.

They hadn't made it past the small foyer when the shit hit the fan.

Isaiah heard the sound of someone rummaging around instantly, but before he could send Cassidy and Micah back out, the gunman sauntered out of one of the rooms, his gun trained on Isaiah.

"You might wanna lower the weapon," Isaiah said calmly, the barrel of his own .45 aimed right between the guy's eyes.

"This ain't your fight," the masked intruder declared.

"No?" Isaiah countered, giving the room a quick once-over before returning his gaze to the man's gun. "A little late for that, huh?"

"Hand over the girl and we'll be on our way."

We? Shit.

There were more of them?

Without another second's thought, Isaiah double-checked his aim and pulled the slide back, sending one into the chamber. Unlike the idiot holding him at gunpoint, Isaiah didn't plan to stand there and have a polite conversation. Which was why he pulled the trigger, then turned and shoved Cassidy and Micah toward the door.

"Go!" he commanded when Micah pulled the door open. Isaiah pushed Cassidy into the hall behind his brother. "Run and don't fucking stop!"

"You shot him!" Cassidy said, as though he weren't already aware of that fact.

He opted not to say anything, knowing she wouldn't understand.

A second later, a gunshot rang out from behind them, and the only thing Isaiah could hope was that the second guy was a bad shot. Cassidy screamed, but he nudged her forward, taking her directly to the stairwell.

"Lose the shoes," he commanded as he shoved the door inward, causing it to slam against the concrete wall.

"But—"

Isaiah didn't give her a chance to argue. He pulled her up short, yanking the damn heels from her feet and tossing them behind him.

"Now fucking run."

Micah grabbed her hand and pulled her with him down the stairs. Isaiah followed them.

They hadn't made it far when the door above them opened, but thankfully, the stairwell wrapped around a concrete wall, which left them covered. Didn't mean they'd escape, since Cassidy wasn't moving fast enough for his peace of mind, but it was all they had, so he'd take it.

He heard the man gaining on them by the time they hit the third floor. They weren't nearly low enough to get away before the asshole caught up, so he decided on a detour.

"Micah!" Isaiah called.

When his brother glanced over his shoulder, Isaiah nodded toward the door.

Micah's nod said his brother understood what he wanted to do. Grabbing the metal handle, Micah pulled the door open and instructed Cassidy to go into the hallway.

There they both grabbed her arms and ran toward the opposite end.

Since the condo split out into three hallways, Isaiah knew there was another stairwell for safety. He only hoped the asshole gunning for them didn't realize where they'd gone until it no longer mattered.

It only took another few minutes for them to make it back down to the ground floor. Isaiah took Cassidy's shaking hand in his and pretended a casualness he didn't feel as they stepped out into the Vegas sunshine through the emergency exit.

"I don't have shoes on," Cassidy informed them when they stepped onto the pavement.

"The car's over there," Isaiah told her quickly. "You'll survive."

Isaiah pretended not to hear her when she grunted at his remark. There was a guy shooting at them, and she was worried about her feet. He would never understand women. Nor was he going to try.

"Where're we going?" she questioned when Micah was pulling his Dodge Challenger out of the parking lot.

"Back to the hotel. More specifically, our club." That way they didn't have to worry about anything. Isaiah knew for a fact that no one was stupid enough to fuck with Max Adorite, especially on his own turf. "You'll be safe there."

"What's the name of this club, anyway?"

"Devil's Playground," Micah inserted. "Heard of it?"

Of course she'd heard of it. Anyone from Vegas knew of Devil's Playground, but Isaiah didn't say as much.

Cassidy snorted, a disbelieving sound that drew Isaiah's attention.

"Problem?"

"No, it just seems aptly named, that's all," she said snidely.

If she only knew.

Micah took the back roads to the center of the strip and then pulled into the private parking garage, where only a few were allowed to park their vehicles. It was an extra security measure Max had insisted on. Regardless of how well the club did, how many people lined up for miles to get in, Devil's Playground was still owned by an organized crime syndicate, and that alone meant extra security measures were needed. Then again, most of Vegas was owned by the mob and always had been. Since Max had recently acquired the hotel and casino, it went without saying that he could do whatever the hell he wanted.

And now Isaiah only hoped the man had a plan, because they'd just added homicide to the list of reasons the bad guys were after Cassidy.

10

CASSIDY WASN'T SURE exactly who Isaiah was talking to, but she had a good idea when he said, "Here with me. We're back at the club. But we've got a problem. One guy dead in her condo, another still looking for her."

A dead guy. She'd watched it happen. Watched as Isaiah had calmly shot and killed another man right in front of her.

She could only assume Max's response to that.

Placing the phone on speaker, Isaiah leaned back in his chair. Cassidy could sense his tension, despite the fact that he appeared nonchalant—as though he were unaffected by the fact that he'd killed someone.

She doubted anyone could be unaffected.

They'd retreated to a small, expensively decorated office in the club. While Micah had paced the floor and Isaiah had gone right for his cell phone, Cassidy had taken the opportunity to admire the room.

The walls were covered in dark wood with the exception of one wall of windows that overlooked the north end of the strip. A large, mahogany desk took up the center of the room, along with a credenza that held several decanters of liquor and some empty glasses. Other than a couple of chairs, a well-secured safe in one wall, and another door that appeared to lead to a private bathroom, there wasn't much else to look at.

"Did someone call it in?" Max asked from the phone Isaiah had placed on his desk.

"No idea. We hauled ass out of there. My guess is no since the silencer muted the sound."

"Send a cleanup crew. Have Jake oversee it." Max continued with his instructions on what Isaiah needed to do to handle the problem. When that was out of the way, Isaiah disconnected the call.

"What now?" Cassidy asked.

Isaiah shrugged.

Great. He had no idea what they were supposed to do now, and he'd just killed a man.

Granted, she knew that if Isaiah hadn't pulled the trigger, he'd probably be the dead one and she'd be in the hands of God knew who.

That didn't make her feel any better.

"I'll call Jake and get things taken care of," Micah informed them.

Cassidy turned her attention to Isaiah's twin, noticing the severe expression on his face. He didn't bother to look at her, and she no longer wondered whether or not he was fond of her. She was certain he wasn't.

Not that she could necessarily blame him. She'd inadvertently brought danger to their doorstep.

"Let me know if you need anything," Isaiah replied. "And Micah, keep your eyes open."

Micah nodded to Isaiah and then left.

"So what now?" Cassidy asked when they were alone.

Isaiah's intense gaze lifted to meet hers, and she realized she was shaking. The adrenaline had run its course, and she couldn't stop the overwhelming chill that took up residence in her bones.

"Come here," Isaiah said firmly.

Cassidy's feet had a mind of their own, moving toward him at the instruction.

When she was within reach, Isaiah's arms lifted, and the next thing she knew, she was in his lap, his strong arms wrapped around her.

"I'm gonna keep you safe," he whispered, his breath fanning her hair as she buried her face against his chest.

She prayed that was true, though she would never tell him as much. She wasn't fond of having someone take care of her. She'd been doing a fairly decent job all these years. It kind of sucked that she had to lean on someone else at this point.

Regardless, she couldn't stop trembling, even as she allowed Isaiah's warmth and strength to surround her.

Several minutes passed as they remained like that, with her in his lap, his arms banded around her, his chin resting on top of her head. Finally feeling somewhat more at ease, Cassidy lifted her head and looked at him.

For whatever reason—she blamed her out-of-control nerves—her gaze strayed to his mouth, and she had the sudden urge to kiss him.

"Cassidy."

The way he said her name, the deep, dark rumble of his voice, sent a frisson of heat through her, effectively warming her from the inside out.

Without thinking, Cassidy leaned in and pressed her lips to his, not caring if he pushed her away.

He didn't.

No, Isaiah didn't push her away; instead, he seemed to pull her closer. Cassidy wrapped her arms around his neck, her fingers sliding through the silky strands of his dark hair as he took control of the kiss, his tongue sliding into her mouth when she opened to him.

Her body quivered in response, but this had nothing to do with fear and everything to do with desire, need.

Giving in to the kiss, Cassidy practically tried to climb his body, although he was holding her firmly in his lap. She wanted to get closer, to feel every part of him against every part of her. His big palm spread across her back, holding her so that her breasts were crushed to the solid plane of his chest.

"Be careful, little girl," Isaiah breathed, a clear warning in his tone.

For the first time in her life, Cassidy didn't want to be careful. She wanted to throw caution to the wind, to forget all the shit taking place around her. She wanted to get lost in this man.

So, that was exactly what she decided to do.

11

ISAIAH WASN'T SURE what had gotten into Cassidy, but he was hard-pressed to resist her. She was ablaze, fire in his arms, and he was tempted. So goddamn tempted.

She tasted sweet, like candy mixed with sin. A taste he was finding himself quickly addicted to.

He liked the fact that she was kissing him, taking the reins, although they both knew he was in total control. Yet he couldn't bring himself to pull away, despite the fact that he'd warned her.

When her lips trailed down his jaw to his neck, Isaiah closed his eyes. "In about two seconds, I'm going to pick you up and carry you into that bathroom. Then I'm going to strip us both naked." Isaiah cupped the back of her head, holding her close as she continued to trail a blaze of fire over his skin. "At that point, we're going to get in that shower, and I'm going to fuck you right up against the wall. Is that what you want, Cassidy?"

To his surprise, she pulled back but didn't try to get away. No, she remained where she was, leaning far enough that she could look into his eyes.

"Yes," she said firmly, her tone reflecting the heat he could feel radiating from her body. "That's what I want."

No one had to tell him twice.

With a surge of adrenaline, Isaiah was out of the chair, Cassidy still in his arms. With ease, he carried her into the bathroom and kicked the door shut.

After turning on the water so it had time to warm, he did exactly as he'd promised, stripping them both, never taking his hands off Cassidy for longer than a second. Luckily, he managed to think of their safety, retrieving a condom from his wallet and tossing it on the counter within reach.

Beneath that tank top and shorts, she was perfection. Her smooth, creamy skin was flushed with desire, her eyes glazed with passion. And she seemed as desperate to touch him as he was to touch her.

"Cassidy." He breathed her name as he cupped her head, pulling her lips back to his.

"No more warnings," she whispered, taking the reins once again as she pulled him into the shower with her.

The hot water cascaded over them while Isaiah filled his palms with her breasts, squeezing gently until she moaned. He continued to thrust his tongue into her mouth while he pressed her against the tiled wall, unable to get enough of her. His cock ached, throbbing painfully between them as he anticipated burying himself inside her, lodging himself deep until she was crying out his name in ecstasy.

When her fingers wrapped around his erection, he nearly swallowed his tongue. It was heaven and hell combined, so damn perfect but not nearly enough to satisfy him.

"Stroke me," he growled, nipping her bottom lip.

Cassidy did as he asked, her soft fingers wrapping around him, gliding up and down with just enough pressure to make his eyes cross. Pulling back from her, he glanced down between their bodies, watching her as she jacked his dick.

"You like that?" she asked, an innocence in her tone that caused more of his blood to pool south.

"Yeah," he muttered, lifting his eyes to meet hers briefly. "Fuck yeah."

Closing his eyes, he allowed the sensation to overwhelm him. It'd been a long damn time since he'd merely basked in the pleasure of a woman. Generally he would give in to sate the urge, but with Cassidy … for some reason, he wanted more from her. He didn't want it to end.

And that made no fucking sense.

When the pleasure became too much, nearly sending him over the edge before he was ready, Isaiah gripped her wrist, stilling her. Her eyes widened as she peered up at him.

Wanting to taste her, to give her as much pleasure as she was giving him, Isaiah went to his knees in front of her. "Put your leg on my shoulder," he instructed.

She clutched his hair as she lifted her leg, propping herself up and open to his hungry gaze. Using his fingers, he separated her soft pink folds, admiring her momentarily before he leaned forward and slid his tongue through her slickness.

"Isaiah!"

Cassidy's cry spurred him on. Isaiah forced his tongue into her tight entrance, a burst of pain igniting in his spine when she gripped his hair tightly.

"Isaiah! I… Oh… Please don't stop!"

Using his tongue to tease her clit, Isaiah thrust one finger inside her, fucking her gently. She was so tight, so wet.

He wanted her to come all over his fucking tongue.

He held her upright, allowing her to ride his fingers while he sucked her clit, flicking the engorged bundle of nerves with his tongue until she was panting and moaning, begging him to send her over.

When Cassidy came … he was awestruck. He'd never seen anything more beautiful than this woman in the throes of an intense orgasm. She was mesmerizing.

And clearly eager for more.

She gripped his arms, pulling him until he was forced to get back to his feet.

"Condom," she said, grabbing his head and pulling his mouth to hers.

After kissing her briefly, he turned, fumbled outside the shower for the condom he'd placed there. Once he retrieved it, he didn't waste time. Within seconds he was sheathed.

Cassidy was trembling as she desperately tried to climb his body. Knowing she would rob him of his strength the instant his dick slid inside her, Isaiah opted to sit on the marble ledge, dragging her with him.

"Turn around," he commanded.

She turned to face away from him, and Isaiah pulled her down onto his lap, easing his cock inside her as she situated herself, her legs spread wide.

"Fuck," he groaned when her body sheathed him, pulling him in deep.

Cassidy's hand came around, pulling his head forward so that they were cheek to cheek. She turned her head back so that he could meet her mouth.

Thrusting his tongue inside, he inhaled her moans as he filled her pussy with his cock. With one hand on her hip, guiding her up and down on him, impaling her over and over, unable to go slow, Isaiah used his other hand to tease her clit.

"More," she pleaded. "Harder."

Isaiah broke the kiss, nipping her shoulder with his teeth as he thrust his hips upward, driving into her, his thighs burning from the effort, but it was so fucking worth it.

"Cass," he breathed. "You're so fucking tight."

Cassidy moved, closing her legs, which locked her muscles along his shaft, driving him to the precipice almost instantly. Restraining himself, he managed to hold off by stilling her. He wasn't ready to come. Not yet. The pleasure was more than he'd bargained for, and he never wanted it to end.

"Stand up," he insisted, guiding her up with his hips and his hands until he was standing behind her.

Planting his palm on her back, he urged her forward. "Put your hands on the wall."

When she did, Isaiah gripped her hips again and began pounding inside her, watching as the water sprayed down on her slender back, her coppery hair dark as it hung down over her shoulders.

"I want you to come for me, Cass. And when you do, I want you to say my name."

Cassidy moaned.

"Hear me?" he asked when she didn't respond.

"Yes," she said breathlessly, slamming her hips back against him, forcing him deeper.

With a slight adjustment, Isaiah changed the angle, fucking her hard and fast. He needed her to come before he did, but at the rate they were going, he wasn't sure that was possible.

She'd done something to him, affected him in a way he hadn't expected, and unlike with any woman who'd come before her, Isaiah wasn't sure he'd ever get enough of Cassidy Owens.

"Isaiah! Oh, God. I'm …"

Her body tightened around him, and then she screamed, his name tumbling from her lips, pulling his release from him.

"Fuck, baby." His guttural roar echoed in the bathroom, but he didn't care.

And just as he'd expected, he was sated in a way he'd never experienced before.

But no matter how good it was, he wasn't sure it would last long.

Which meant he needed to get her out of that shower as fast as possible.

12

FEELING COMPLETELY BONELESS, Cassidy allowed Isaiah to wash her after they… She wasn't even sure what to call what they'd just done. Making love? Fucking? Water sports?

It wasn't that she was naïve and thought that whenever a man and a woman came together in such an explosive way it was making love, but for her, there was something … special about what had just happened between her and Isaiah.

Whether he felt the same, she didn't know, and she certainly didn't have any plans to ask him.

Instead, she caught her breath while he tended to her every need. Once they were both clean, Isaiah wrapped her in a giant, fluffy navy blue towel and helped her out of the shower.

"Let's go back to my place," he told her.

Glancing down at herself, Cassidy smiled. "I'm not sure I'm dressed for the occasion."

"I've got a private elevator," he informed her, tucking his own towel around his narrow hips.

Cassidy's gaze locked on that sexy V that formed beneath his washboard abs.

The man truly was an amazing specimen. With clothes, he was stunning; without … well, without clothes, he was sexy as hell.

As though he were reading her mind, Isaiah grinned and pulled her in close.

"Think you can refrain until we're in bed?"

Cassidy nodded, feeling a rush of embarrassment flood her cheeks. Ogling a naked man wasn't something she'd done before. Turned out that Isaiah brought out a side of her that she hadn't known even existed. He made her want to get in tune with her baser urges, her carnal fantasies.

And it wasn't helping that he was practically naked and touching her.

Isaiah chuckled as he took her hand and led her back into his office. He moved across the room to what appeared to be a wall but turned out to be a well-hidden elevator door. Within minutes, they were back in his penthouse. More accurately, they were in his bed.

Without warning, Isaiah tugged her towel loose and tossed it on the floor along with his. In one quick move, Cassidy found herself flat on her back with Isaiah's warm weight hovering above her.

His mouth found hers, and an involuntary moan escaped her. She couldn't help herself. Isaiah Fontenot was the best kisser in the entire world. She'd never kissed a man who could so easily control the kiss, making her want more, with just his lips and tongue.

"I need to taste you again," he grumbled, the vibration from his chest making her nipples harden.

"If you're looking for me to stop you, it won't happen," she retorted playfully.

"Good," he said, meeting her gaze. "Put your hands on the headboard. And don't move them."

Cassidy did as instructed, grabbing the wooden headboard with her fingertips while Isaiah's mouth trailed over her jaw, her neck, her chest.

When he stopped over her breast, his tongue slid sensually over her nipple as she watched. He blew against her skin, sending a delightful shiver dancing down her spine. Her sex clenched and her body ached for him.

"Don't stop," she said.

Isaiah's smirk was devastating.

But it left as quickly as it'd come, and the next thing Cassidy knew, Isaiah sucked her nipple into his mouth, using his teeth and tongue to tease and torment her until she was squirming beneath him, desperately trying to get closer.

She barely managed to catch her breath when he switched to her other nipple, his fingers joining in the mix as he teased her clit with his thumb.

"Isaiah. Oh, please. Please!"

"Please, what?"

"Make me come."

"With my fingers? Or my mouth?"

She didn't care, as long as she reached that pinnacle that was just out of reach.

"Everything," she responded.

Another chuckle rumbled from him, and then Isaiah moved lower, his tongue gliding over her skin, then zeroing in right where she needed him most. Without fanfare, Isaiah flicked her clit relentlessly, driving her crazy as her orgasm built, starting in her core and radiating outward right before it … exploded!

"Yes! Oh, God, yes!"

Before she came back to herself, Isaiah was hovering over her once more, his thick erection, sheathed in a condom he'd miraculously produced, prodding at her opening. Wrapping her legs around his waist, Cassidy released the headboard, gripped his ass, and pulled him forward until he was seated inside her, filling her completely.

He stretched her deliciously, his mouth settling over hers.

And then the intensity shifted, turning into something much more passionate, deeper than anything she'd ever felt. He was moving languorously, sliding in deep and retreating, lighting up every sensitive nerve ending along the way.

Being with him was perfection, and Cassidy never wanted it to end. She wanted to ride the wave of ecstasy for as long as possible.

Isaiah's arm slid beneath her, holding her tight to his chest as he rolled them, effectively placing Cassidy on top of him. The change in angle sent a shiver down her spine.

"Ride me," he instructed, that no-nonsense tone causing her muscles to spasm, tightening around his cock lodged deep inside her.

Sitting up, Cassidy placed her hands on Isaiah's chest, sliding her fingers through the soft, dark hair as she rocked her hips, taking the reins and fucking him as slowly as he'd been fucking her. Their eyes met, locked as she continued to control their pleasure.

"So beautiful," Isaiah whispered, his voice raspy with desire.

It sent a surge of feminine power through her that caught her off guard.

Yes, there was something uniquely different about this man. She'd known him for less than a full day, and yet Cassidy wanted so many more days with him. Days she would use to explore whatever this was between them.

Hell, if she didn't know better, she'd think she could possibly fall in love with him.

Just sex. Sex doesn't equal love.

Shaking off the thought, Cassidy lost herself in the moment, giving in to the fantasy that this could potentially be more than that. More than just sex.

13

ISAIAH WAS CLOSE. So fucking close. And it wasn't easy to hold back while watching Cassidy ride him, her sweet pussy gripping him, her beautiful breasts swaying as she fucked him.

But there was something else, something more than her sexy body that mesmerized him. The way she watched him, as though he were the only man in the entire world… It did something to him … something he wasn't ready to come to terms with just yet.

"That's it, Cass. Fuck me, baby. Come for me."

Holding her hips, Isaiah regained control, bucking his hips upward, fucking her deep and hard. Her damp hair fell over them like a silk curtain when she leaned forward, her beautiful green eyes still locked with his.

He continued with the torturous pace until her eyes slid shut, her lips parted slightly.

That was when he recanted his original thought. Right then, as her orgasm erupted, Cassidy was by far the sexiest, most desirable woman in the entire world.

Holding her hips, he focused on fucking her, wanting to send her over once more. He drove in deep, holding her still while he lifted his hips, then jerking her onto him when he was buried to the hilt. Over and over, faster, harder, deeper. He didn't stop until his body ignited, a sizzling tingle starting in the base of his spine.

"Fuck," he growled as his release detonated, his hips stilling as he held her, burying himself as deep as he could get, only wishing he could go even deeper.

Minutes later, after he'd cleaned up and they'd both managed to catch their breath, Isaiah curled up behind Cassidy in his bed, holding her tight to his body.

"We should sleep," he mumbled, his eyes already heavy from exhaustion.

"I agree," Cassidy whispered.

And that was the last he remembered before sleep overtook him.

☒☒☒☒

Isaiah woke to the sound of his cell phone ringing. When he opened his eyes, he noticed that the room was dark, and it wasn't because the heavy, room-darkening curtains were closed. A quick glance at the clock told him it was after eight, which meant they'd slept for a while.

Releasing his hold on Cassidy, he managed to roll over and grab his phone before it went to voice mail.

"Hello?" he greeted, his voice rough from sleep.

"Rise and shine, sleeping beauty."

"What do you want?" he asked his brother, not bothering to hide his irritation at being woken.

"Well, I figured you'd want to know that I found her brother."

Isaiah abruptly sat up in the bed, peering over at Cassidy. Her eyes opened as though she'd heard what Micah had said.

"What is it?" she asked, pulling the sheet up to cover her naked breasts.

"Is she … in your bed?" Micah asked, disbelief ringing in his words.

Isaiah chose to ignore the question. "Where is he?" Isaiah asked Micah while keeping his eyes on Cassidy.

"He's holed up at the Golden Nugget."

"Fucking seriously?" Isaiah figured the guy at least had the brains to get out of town.

"What?" Cassidy asked, her eyes wide as she sat up. Clearly she knew they were talking about her.

"Micah found your brother. He's still here in Vegas."

"Is he…?"

"Yeah, he's alive," Isaiah told her, hating the fear he saw in her eyes. Turning his attention back to Micah, he added, "Give us half an hour. We'll meet you in my office."

"Already a *we*? What the hell are you thinking, Isaiah?"

Once again, Isaiah ignored his brother.

Micah huffed, then said, "Whatever. You want me to go pick him up?"

"No. We'll take Cassidy to him. Maybe keep him from running."

"Good plan. See you in thirty."

Isaiah disconnected the call and reached for Cassidy. She was shaking, and that bothered him more than it should. Cupping the back of her head, he forced her to look at him. "He's fine. We won't let anything happen to him. But we need to get dressed and get down there before someone else finds him."

Cassidy nodded. “I need something to wear.”

Shit. Isaiah thought back to their trip to her condo. It hadn’t ended the way he’d anticipated. They hadn’t gotten any of her things, and on top of that, he’d killed someone.

Surprisingly, he didn’t care about the latter. If it meant protecting Cassidy, he’d do it a million times over without an ounce of regret.

“I’ll make a call. Get someone to grab something from the boutique downstairs.”

Another nod from Cassidy.

Isaiah watched her for a moment. Finding her brother was the first step to ending this for her, the first milestone they needed to surpass in order to get her back to her normal life, to keeping her safe.

That didn’t explain why he was suddenly reluctant to let her go.

14

CASSIDY TUGGED AT the sundress she was wearing. It wasn't that it didn't fit, because it did, but that didn't mean it was comfortable. Maybe it was because she wasn't really a sundress kind of girl. Or perhaps she was just irritable because she wanted to see her brother and they'd yet to leave the hotel.

After Isaiah had called someone to get her something to wear, he had hopped into the shower once again and then dressed quickly. After the outfit had arrived—a white number with yellow flowers—Cassidy had changed and then they'd taken the private elevator back down to Isaiah's office at the club, where they'd met Micah.

At that point, she'd thought they were heading out, but Isaiah had opted to call Max, who he was currently on the phone with. She couldn't hear what they were saying because Isaiah had taken the phone and retreated to the other room. Clearly he wanted to have a private conversation, and that bothered her. This was about her brother. Didn't she deserve to hear what was going on?

"You ready?"

At the sound of Isaiah's voice, Cassidy launched to her feet, meeting his stern gaze from across the room.

Without another word, the three of them headed out through the club's main entrance. Once they were at the hotel's VIP exit, they were met by two additional men.

"Cassidy, this is Jake Andrews and Hayden Wellington. They work for Max."

The men spared her a quick glance and a polite nod, but no one said anything, which was fine by her. She was ready to get the show on the road.

As the five of them stepped outside, Cassidy realized why the other men were there. They were added protection, evident when she found herself flanked on all sides by four oversized men. All four of them armed.

They didn't separate until she was safely inside a shiny black Cadillac Escalade. At that point, they joined her quickly, then they headed out.

Micah was obviously familiar with Vegas, because the trip downtown didn't take long, mainly because he avoided all of the heavily traveled roads. He opted for valet parking, which surprised her considering she'd have opted for a quick getaway. Unless they knew something she didn't, that wasn't going to happen.

But she didn't question them.

They continued in silence into the casino entrance.

The Golden Nugget was just as she remembered from the last time she'd visited, which had been nearly a decade ago. It reminded her of classic movies with its old movie style, golden lights shining down from low ceilings, brass fixtures on the walls.

The trek through the hotel was long, but they managed it without incident. Another elevator ride and they were finally on one of the hotel floors. Once again, all four men flanked her, keeping her tightly tucked between their large bodies until they reached what was obviously their destination.

"Knock on the door," Isaiah instructed Cassidy.

He gave her just enough room to knock as well as be seen through the security hole in the door. A second later, the door flew open and there was…

"Fuck," Micah growled as Isaiah pulled Cassidy behind him, effectively shielding her from the two oversized goons and the skinny old man who were guarding Jordan.

Through some strange phenomenon, Cassidy managed to remain calm rather than to fly into a fit of rage when she saw the damage that had been done to her brother. He was tied to a chair, one of his eyes swollen completely shut, his lip busted and bleeding.

"Before you do something you'll regret," the older, gray-haired man sitting in a chair beside Jordan, holding a gun to his head began, "I'd highly suggest we handle this in a civilized manner."

"Civilized?" Isaiah asked with a chuckle that didn't hold an ounce of humor.

The eerie tone of his voice made her stomach churn. There was something distinctly different about him, but she didn't know him well enough to know what that was.

"A little late for that, huh?" Micah asked as both men stepped into the room, leaving Cassidy with Jake and Hayden behind them.

"We're just working through our issues," the man replied casually.

"Well, good. Because we're here to settle this," Isaiah informed the man.

"I see Max has come to his senses."

Isaiah laughed, a dark, threatening sound that made the hair on the back of Cassidy's neck stand on end.

"No, actually. His instructions were simple."

One of the other guys in the room aimed his gun at Jordan's head.

"And that would be?" the gray-haired man inquired.

"Kill you all."

"Well, from where I sit, that doesn't seem beneficial to any of us."

"Maybe not," Isaiah said, his gun at his side. "In the meantime, I brought the money he owes you."

"Good to see Max decided to pay up. Or was it the sister?" the man questioned angrily.

"Oh, she doesn't have anything to do with this."

"Well, I won't accept payment from Max."

"Who said Max would be willing to pay?" Isaiah asked.

Cassidy was hanging by a thread, hating this game they were playing. Was Isaiah bluffing? Or did he really have the money? He'd never mentioned it if he did.

And if he was telling the truth, the next questions she had were: Where was the money, and how were they planning to get Jordan out of there alive?

15

HOWARD TURNER WAS a wannabe gangster with a bad temper and an even worse toupee. He was nothing more than a bottom-feeding loan shark who preyed on people like Jordan Owens, a man with a gambling problem living in the wrong city and succumbing to the draw of Sin City.

That didn't mean Isaiah would discount the fact that Howard had a gun and looked ready to blow Cassidy's brother's head right off.

But Isaiah knew the man wouldn't do as much because without Jordan Owens alive, there was no reason for anyone to settle his debt. And Isaiah hadn't been kidding when he'd shared Max's orders to kill them all. That was the plan.

Maybe not today, but it would happen.

Max Adorite didn't play games, and when he asked nicely for someone to reach out to him, this wasn't how he meant. And for that, Howard Turner would die.

However, Isaiah's goal was to get Jordan out of there in one piece, reunite him with his sister, and get the Owens siblings back to life as normal.

"I take it you received Max's request," Isaiah questioned, his gaze scanning the room, taking it all in.

"I did. I figured this was a good way to let him know I wasn't playing his little game."

"Oh, Max doesn't play games," Isaiah assured Howard. "Then again, you already knew that."

There was true fear in Howard Turner's light brown eyes. He knew he'd crossed a line. Granted, he likely had a plan of his own, and Isaiah hoped he would get to hear about it.

He smiled when Howard spoke.

"I don't have a beef with Max Adorite," Howard said, his eyes locked with Isaiah's.

"You mean, you didn't. Until today," Isaiah added. "The bottom line is, Mr. Turner, I'm here to take Jordan Owens. Alive."

"He's not going anywhere until I get my money."

"I don't have your money," Jordan grumbled.

"So you've said," Howard retorted with a disgusting grin. "Doesn't mean you won't come up with it. I've already told you, we'll take that pretty sister of yours as collateral."

Isaiah growled. The thought of Howard putting his filthy hands on what belonged to him didn't sit well.

Wait.

Belonged to him?

Since when had he claimed Cassidy as his own?

Before he had a chance to ponder that question, Howard spoke again.

"So what'll it be?"

Isaiah lifted his eyebrow, encouraging Howard to tell him the options.

"I'll take the thirty-five thousand that Mr. Owens owes me right now, and you can have him back. Or …"

"Or?" Isaiah asked, trying to keep his cool.

"Or we can make a trade until Mr. Owens can come up with the money."

"Not gonna happen," Isaiah assured him. "I've got thirty. You take it, hand over Jordan, and you can be on your merry way. Otherwise, you don't have shit, and in about thirty seconds, I'll have the cash and the kid."

That got Harold's attention. He got to his feet and righted his suit jacket, never taking his eyes off Isaiah.

"Thirty isn't the deal. I said thirty-five."

"That's not what he owes you."

"Sure it is. I charge for my time, and I've wasted the last half hour on him. That's an extra five."

Isaiah shook his head. "Thirty or no deal. Your choice. But keep in mind, the more you barter, the deeper of a hole you dig yourself. You claim you don't have a beef with Mr. Adorite, but you seem to forget who you're dealing with. Continue on this path, and he'll have a beef with *you.* He asked nicely for you to reach out to him, to talk this through. You opted to ignore his generosity."

"What's keeping me from getting the rest of my money from the sister?" Harold questioned, his tone hard, his gaze backlit with fury.

"Because you touch one hair on her head and I'll rip your throat out with my bare hands," Isaiah said, his tone lethal. "Understood?"

Harold glanced over at Jordan, seemingly weighing his options.

Isaiah knew better.

People underestimated him, figured him to be a street-stupid businessman. What most people didn't realize was that Isaiah had never had it easy. He could brawl with the best of them, even at thirty-eight.

And the last thing he would tolerate was anyone threatening to hurt a woman. Especially *his* woman.

Shrugging off the thought once again, Isaiah said, "Like I said. Your choice. I've got a club to run, and I'm wasting my time with you. So either choose the money so we can all be on our way or don't. I don't really give a fuck."

Howard's cheeks puffed up, his anger apparent. "Fuck you, Fontenot. Give me the goddamn money, but I hope you realize this ain't over."

Isaiah reached for the brown bag that Jake had brought with him. He then tossed it over to Harold.

When everyone's eyes were on the bag in the air, Hayden slipped into the room, his movements not noticed until it was too late. With Hayden's gun now pointed at Harold's head, Isaiah instructed Harold's men to untie Jordan.

"It's all over, kids. Toss your guns on the floor or Mr. Wellington won't hesitate to off your boss."

Isaiah spared Harold a glance.

"Do it," Harold ordered.

"Smart move," he told Harold, then turned his attention back to the man closest to Jordan. "Let him go and you can have your boss back. Don't make this any harder than it has to be."

Harold snarled at Isaiah but instructed his men to release Jordan.

Minutes later, Harold and his guys were on their way out of the room, their guns still on the floor, while Cassidy and Jordan reunited.

It was then that Isaiah breathed a sigh of relief.

Right before he began pondering the questions he'd had earlier.

Not that he knew how to answer them, but he figured he was running out of time, so he had to do something quick, before Cassidy Owens simply waltzed right out of his life as fast as she'd waltzed in.

16

CASSIDY HAD MANAGED to keep it together after Isaiah had diffused the situation, during their uneventful trip back to Devil's Playground, and even long enough for some man who claimed he was a doctor to check Jordan out in Isaiah's office.

But that didn't last long when Isaiah confronted her while her brother was talking on the phone with Max and Courtney Adorite.

"You okay?" Isaiah asked, his voice soft, soothing, as though he was truly concerned about her well-being.

He placed his finger beneath her chin and tilted her head back, forcing her to look at him. That was when Cassidy lost it.

Throwing her arms around Isaiah's waist, she held on to him, every ounce of the fear she'd had when they'd found her brother tied to a chair and beaten rushing out of her in a flood of tears.

"Hey," Isaiah crooned against her ear. "Everything's fine now."

"I know," she sobbed.

But she didn't know.

Sure, Jordan was alive, and his debt with that man had been settled, but there was still the fact that someone had paid off his debt, which meant he wasn't out of the hot seat. And it also left Cassidy wondering where she and Isaiah stood. Now that she was safe, would he simply walk away?

Did she want more from him?

Did it even matter?

It took a minute for her to master her resolve, but Cassidy finally reined in the tears, forcing herself to get a firm grip on her emotions.

Isaiah pulled back and looked down at her. Wiping her face with the heels of her hands, Cassidy hoped she didn't look as bad as she felt.

"The club's going to open in a few minutes. I need to get out there."

"Is it safe for me to go home?" she asked.

Isaiah didn't respond immediately, making her wonder what he was thinking about.

"Not yet," he finally said. "There're a couple of loose ends that Jake and Hayden are taking care of now. You can stay with me tonight?"

The last sentence was posed as a question, and Cassidy clung to the hope that had filled her chest earlier that day when they'd made love in his bed. Nodding her agreement, she tried to take a step back.

"Until then, I want you to come to work with me tonight. Will you do that?"

That question surprised her. "I don't have anything to wear."

"If we go right now, you can pick something out at the boutique."

Cassidy couldn't find any reason to argue with him. She wanted to spend more time with him, especially if they would be going their separate ways soon. For a woman who was known for her level-headedness, she knew her reaction to Isaiah was anything but. However, she had a valid reason... She simply didn't want their time together to end.

Sliding her hand into his, Cassidy forced a smile as she peered up into his beautiful brown eyes. "Okay."

An hour later, Cassidy was walking through the club, hand in hand with Isaiah as he greeted people, taking the time to actually talk to the VIP guests one on one, ensuring they were having a good time and checking to see if they needed anything.

It was surreal, his job. Isaiah was toe-to-toe with the rich and famous. There were so many people that Cassidy recognized from popular movies, plenty of music stars, all shoulder to shoulder with Isaiah, treating him as though he were their best friend while they all had a good time at Devil's Playground.

Sure, she'd heard of the place but had never been, even though she'd lived in Vegas her entire life. Although the club was nice—nicer than nice, actually—it still wasn't her thing. Sure, she liked the setup, the fancy water features that flowed throughout, the various seating areas, the LED lighting that gave the place a sexy, almost romantic feel, but it wouldn't have been her first choice for a night out.

She had to admit, despite that, she was having a good time with Isaiah. He politely introduced her to everyone he spoke with, seemingly proud that she was there with him. It gave her a sense of belonging that she hadn't felt in so long.

Not once during the night did she worry about Jordan. She knew he was there, still being protected by Isaiah's bodyguards because they had some unfinished business to attend to tomorrow. No, her entire focus was on Isaiah. As though she were taking it all in, memorizing every physical detail so that she could hang on to it when this was all over.

"Your brother asked to speak with you," Isaiah told her as he led her toward a set of stairs. "I'll give you two a few minutes."

Cassidy nodded and then ascended the stairs when Isaiah motioned her up.

When she reached the second floor, her eyes took a moment to focus in the dark, but then she noticed Jordan sitting at a table near the wall. As she approached, he got to his feet, pulling her into a hug as soon as she was close enough.

"Thank you," he whispered against her ear.

"For?" she asked, pulling back and looking at him.

His face was still puffy, but his eye was no longer swollen shut. It was clear he'd showered and changed.

When Jordan motioned for her to sit down, Cassidy pulled the spare chair closer to him, then eased into it.

"Are you really okay?" she asked, sensing a nervous tension in her brother.

"I will be," he told her, his gaze darting around the area as though he were seeking someone.

"When?"

"When what?" he countered.

"When will you be okay?"

"When this is all settled," he said simply. "I'm supposed to meet with Isaiah tomorrow. Then I'll be having a conversation with Max Adorite." Jordan's eyes searched the area once more before settling on her. "Do you know who these people are, Cass?"

"Yes," she answered simply.

"You realize you've gotten involved with the mafia?" he asked incredulously.

Cassidy leaned closer. "You realize the *mafia* saved your ass today?"

"I know that," he replied, a frustrated hint to his tone. "And I'm grateful. But I don't think you should be mixed up with them."

"Too late for that," she told him.

"Cass—"

"No," she interrupted. "Don't go all big brother on me, Jordan. I know who these people are. And in case you don't remember, it's your fault I'm involved at all. So, spare me the good advice. I don't need it."

Jordan's face fell and Cassidy knew she'd hurt him. As much as she hated that fact, she couldn't see any other way to deal with her brother at the moment. He was always willing to give advice but never seemed to take any. At this point, he still had some debts to settle, and she only hoped Max would be lenient with him.

"So what now?" he asked, his gaze never leaving the table.

"We get back to normal life. And you…" Cassidy waited until he looked at her. "You get some help."

Jordan nodded, but she didn't see sincerity in his gaze. She knew him, knew he'd be the first to make a dozen promises, but he never followed through on them. This time, because he had gotten in with the mafia—as he referred to them—he wasn't going to have much of a choice.

"Don't make any promises," she said before he could speak. "We'll get through this together, okay?"

Jordan nodded, his eyes widening as though he was happy with the idea of her helping him.

A warm hand landed on her shoulder, and Cassidy turned to see Isaiah standing beside her. She smiled up at him, then got to her feet. Glancing back at Jordan, she smiled. "I get to make the promises this time."

Allowing Isaiah to lead her away from the table, Cassidy felt a weight lift off her shoulders. She wasn't going to worry about Jordan right now. He was right where he needed to be, and she knew he was looking for a way out, but Isaiah wouldn't allow that to happen. Not until they settled their business. In the meantime, it would give him time to think things through. Her brother wasn't usually so selfish, but he did have a problem. A problem that she vowed to help him through as long as he was willing. And now that he was in the position he was in, she didn't think he had much of a choice.

So for now, she decided to let the heavy thoughts go. There'd be plenty of time to deal with those later.

"You ready for a break?" Isaiah asked suddenly.

Cassidy turned to look at Isaiah, realizing for the first time that they'd stopped in a relatively quiet corridor on the second floor of the club.

"Sure," she told him, not certain what he had in mind.

The smile he shot back at her made her toes curl. It was a promise.

"Where are we going?" she asked as he led her down the hall.

"My office."

Less than a minute later, that was exactly where they were. His office.

Alone.

Isaiah flipped the lock on the door and stalked her, forcing her back until her butt hit the edge of his desk.

"Have I told you how hot you look in this dress?" he asked.

Cassidy shook her head but added a flirty smile. He had told her, right after she'd put it on. At the time, she'd seen the gleam in his eyes, and she'd been proud of her selection. The slinky red number wasn't something she would've picked out on her own, but the woman at the store had told her that it would set off her hair. She'd been right, and when Isaiah had looked at her after she'd changed, the heat she'd seen in his eyes had been proof.

Isaiah's hands slid up her thighs, forcing the short, tight dress higher until the red thong she'd purchased was the only thing separating her sex from his touch.

He stole her breath when he solved that problem, sliding her panties to the side and teasing her labia with his big, warm fingers.

"I've been dying to get inside you again," he told her, his breath warm against her lips, his finger sliding through her slit.

"So why'd you wait so long?" she teased.

Isaiah smiled, the slight shift of his facial muscles reaching all the way to his eyes.

"You're wet," he said. "For me?"

"Only you," she whispered, realizing how true the words were as soon as they were out of her mouth.

It'd been a long time since Cassidy had felt something for a man, something this intense, this all-consuming. She was a cautious woman, but with Isaiah, she lost every ounce of her inhibitions.

And she didn't care.

Everything that had happened in the last twenty-four hours, everything she'd said and done, she was perfectly content with. It didn't matter to her that Isaiah was part of a mafia family, that he had killed a man while protecting her.

If she had to relive it all over again, she wouldn't change a thing.

Without Regret

She didn't have a single regret.

17

ISAIAH HAD BEEN telling the truth when he'd said he was dying to get inside her again. He'd thought about little else since they'd arrived back at the club. And throughout the night, when he had been making the rounds inside Devil's Playground, he had been tempted to pull Cassidy into a dark corner so he could do just that.

Now they had a little privacy, and he wasn't going to wait any longer.

Sliding his finger through her slick folds, Isaiah pushed inside her, fingering her slowly while she moaned sweetly against his mouth.

"You like that? When I finger you?"

"Yes," she said on a breathless moan. "So much."

He did, too. The scent of her, the sexy sounds she made… It went to his head like nothing else.

"Tell me to eat your pussy, Cassidy," he said softly.

"Yes," she replied. "Please."

"Tell me," he insisted, pulling back enough to make eye contact with her. "I want to hear you say it."

"Eat my … pussy," she whispered, her cheeks turning pink.

It was enough, just hearing those dirty words coming from her sweet mouth… Definitely enough.

Crouching in front of her, Isaiah replaced his finger with his tongue, delving through her smooth folds, tasting her, teasing her.

God, he'd never get enough. He could eat her for hours, never stopping, just to hear her moans, to feel her fingers clasping his hair.

As she ground her pussy against his mouth, Isaiah pushed his finger inside her again, then two. Slowly fucking her while he suckled her clit, looking up at the beautiful woman who had managed, in the matter of a day, to capture a piece of him that he hadn't realized was afloat. But here he was, and this … this few minutes they had to themselves… Isaiah intended to show her how good it could be, because he couldn't see spending tomorrow without her. Or the day after that.

"Isaiah. Oh, God. I need to … feel you … inside me. Fuck me," she cried out, thrusting her hips forward against his intruding fingers while she pulled his hair, urging him back to his feet.

He did as she asked, standing to his full height, retrieving the condom he'd placed in his wallet a short time ago, then releasing his cock and sheathing himself. And then …

Heaven.

He was pushing inside her, her pussy clamping on his dick, squeezing him, milking him, making him crazy with want.

"Cass … you … God, baby, you feel so good," he groaned, burying himself to the hilt in her warmth. "Hold on to me," he ordered.

Cassidy's arms came around his neck, her legs around his hips, her ass perched on the edge of his desk as he began thrusting into her. Harder, faster, deeper.

He feared he would never get enough. Not in this lifetime.

Pulling back to look at her, he locked his gaze with hers. Searching. Seeking.

He wanted to know if what he'd seen there earlier had only been a figment of his imagination.

The way Cassidy's hooded gaze locked with his … he knew she felt it too.

This wasn't just sex. He'd had that enough to know that this was more.

So much more.

"Cassidy… Aww, fuck, baby. Too good."

He thrust his hips forward, slamming into her, holding her with one arm around her back, the other on his desk for traction.

"Harder," Cassidy pleaded. "Never stop, Isaiah. Never."

He didn't intend to, but his body had other ideas. Her muscles tightened around his cock, a surge of pleasure igniting in his veins.

He wanted to fuck her into oblivion, to continue with the punishing thrusts of his hips until she was screaming his name and begging for more.

So. Fucking. Good.

"Isaiah," she breathed, her fingernails digging into his scalp, electrical pulses of pleasure-pain darting down his spine.

"I'm here, Cass. Right here with you, baby." Panting, he continued to thrust into her. "I could do this forever, sinking my dick into your pretty pussy. Aww, that's it, baby. Squeeze my dick."

Her muscles tightened, her breath rushing out of her lungs as she moaned. He was going to come if she kept… Her legs locked tightly around him, the shift of her hips changing the angle, sending him closer to the razor-sharp edge that he hovered over. Crushing his mouth to hers, Isaiah pounded into her, fucking her mercilessly, desperate to make her come.

"Yes," she breathed sharply, breaking the kiss when she tossed her head back. "God, yes!"

Her muscles locked on his cock once more, her legs tightening around his hips as her orgasm crested, sending him right over the edge with her.

Neither of them moved, holding one another until their breathing was somewhat regulated. Even then, Isaiah didn't let her go.

"You okay?" she asked, her fingers sliding through his hair.

"Never better," he whispered, his forehead against her neck.

"So, what do we do now?"

He knew by the tone of her voice that she wasn't talking about cleaning up and going back to work. Cassidy wanted to know about what the future held for them.

Lifting his head and looking directly into her eyes, he swallowed hard. "That's your call."

"Mine? Why mine?"

"I've … never done this before."

Cassidy's smile lit her entire face, and her laugh made him grin.

"You know what I meant," he added.

Her smile faded, her face sobering. "I do know. And I've … never done this before, either."

"There's a first time for everything. Isn't that how the saying goes?"

"I think so," she answered easily.

"Then I say we take this one day at a time."

Her smile returned, and the vise grip on his heart loosened somewhat.

"I like that plan. A lot."

Good. Because he didn't know how else to tell her that he had no intention of walking away.

18

AFTER THEIR RENDEZVOUS in Isaiah's office, Cassidy opted to go to his penthouse while he went back into the club. It was when she was getting presentable in the private bathroom in Isaiah's office that she remembered she had a room at the hotel, which meant she did have some of her things with her.

Why she hadn't thought about it before, she didn't know, but instead of taking the private elevator up to his suite as Isaiah had instructed, Cassidy decided to slip through the club and back to the main part of the hotel. From there, she took the public elevator up to her floor, relieved that things were finally back to normal.

Once inside her hotel room, she took a quick look around, noticing nothing different than the last time she'd been there, which meant during all the chaos, those men who'd taken Jordan hadn't found her hideout. She was grateful for that.

It only took a few minutes for Cassidy to gather her things and to retrieve the items she'd placed in the safe, including the cash she'd pulled out of her savings account in order to try and get Jordan out of his predicament. She'd taken out forty thousand just in case.

It was all there, every bill.

Not that she was all that keen on walking around the casino with that kind of cash, but she didn't have much of a choice. If she wanted to spend one last night with Isaiah before they started taking things one day at a time, she had to get back to his penthouse. Preferably before he realized she'd taken a brief detour.

Dumping all of her bathroom items into her overnight bag, Cassidy finished packing her things. One last look around and she was satisfied that she'd gotten everything.

Just as she was heading to the door, there was a knock. Figuring Isaiah had realized where she'd gone, she smiled to herself as she yanked open the door.

"Ms. Owens. So good to see you again."

Oh, shit.

Cassidy tried to slam the door in the man's face, but he was faster than she was, placing his foot in the way, which kept the door from closing.

Shit. Shit. Shit.

"What do you want?" she asked, trying to keep her cool.

"We've got a few things to discuss, Ms. Owens," the gray-haired man—Mr. Turner, she believed Isaiah had called him—said as he pushed his way into the room.

"I don't think we do," she retorted, clutching her bag close to her side.

"Just so we're clear," the man said, his lips thinning, "I don't give a damn what you think."

When he pulled out his gun, Cassidy knew that her options were extremely limited.

"But we do have somewhere to be, so I suggest you be on your best behavior, and I won't have to hurt you."

Cassidy remembered the conversation from earlier, the clear threat Isaiah had delivered to this man. "Isaiah's going to kill you," she said, using her most lethal tone.

The man merely laughed, which only pissed her off more.

"I think he'll be willing to negotiate. He underestimated me, Ms. Owens. And now he's going to see what I'm truly capable of."

Cassidy did not like the sound of that.

Rather than argue, she allowed him to push her toward the door. Once they were out in the hall, he tucked his gun back into his pants, gripping her arm firmly as he steered her toward the elevator.

If she could get in a public place, surely she could lose him.

Unfortunately, the elevator car that arrived was empty, which meant they were still alone. But not for long.

The elevator delivered them to the main floor a couple of minutes later.

"Think of doing anything stupid and I will shoot you."

Right. Like this idiot was going to shoot her in a crowded casino. A casino owned by Max Adorite, no less.

But she kept that tidbit of information to herself. For now, she'd go willingly.

At least until she found an opening, and that damn sure wouldn't be after they'd made it to their destination.

19

"ISAIAH, WE'VE GOT a problem."

Isaiah stopped his conversation instantly, turning to look at Jake Andrews, the head of security for Devil's Playground and one of Max Adorite's enforcers.

"What is it?" he inquired, watching the man's face intently. The other man did not look happy.

"Ms. Owens never made it back to your penthouse, so I had them search the hotel cameras. She was seen going into one of the rooms a short time ago."

"I'm sure she went to get her things," he said, hoping that was the case. He knew she had been registered at the hotel when he had originally set out to find her.

"Perhaps, but while they watched the cameras, they noticed Howard Turner arrive at her room. A minute later, he left with her at gunpoint."

Fuck.

"We found one of his men here at the club. Apparently he'd been keeping tabs on the two of you."

"Where is he now?"

Jake didn't respond, but the shadows that moved in the man's eyes told Isaiah everything he needed to know. Howard Turner was now down one headcount.

"Where are they?"

"I instructed my men to watch for them on the casino floor. Less than a minute ago, they were seen coming out of the elevator."

"Come with me," Isaiah ordered, making a beeline for the exit.

On his way out, Isaiah gave the bouncer instructions to find Micah, to let him know what was going on, and to have Micah meet him on the casino floor.

Without waiting for his brother, Isaiah allowed Jake to lead him to the area where Howard and Cassidy had been seen last.

That dumb fucker. What was he thinking?

Isaiah knew that was a stupid question. He knew what Howard was thinking. He was going to use Cassidy as a bargaining chip, as a way to get Max off his back.

Too bad Max would never find out about this. Isaiah was more than capable of handling his own. Not to mention, the order to kill Howard had already come down. Looked as though the bastard's timeline had just been moved up.

"There they are," Jake confirmed gruffly. "I'll come around behind them to make sure they don't slip out."

Isaiah nodded, then squeezed through the crowded casino. It was Friday night, and the place was packed. He used the crowd to his advantage, slipping between people while keeping his eyes on Cassidy.

She was carrying a bag, and Howard had a firm grip on her arm. She didn't seem to be trying to get away, which meant she was smart.

He had to wonder whether she knew he'd get to her, that he'd never let anyone hurt her.

Not now. Not ever.

And Howard Turner had just made a grave mistake. One Isaiah fully intended to rectify.

Once he was within a few feet of them, Isaiah opted to use the people scattered about to his benefit. Surely Howard wasn't stupid enough to hurt her in front of all these people. He would know that hotel security would not be lenient on him. They'd shoot first, ask questions later. That was what happened when an armed man attempted to do something stupid in a Vegas casino.

"Cassidy? Hey, honey," he greeted as cheerfully as he could manage. Strolling right up to them, he pulled her into his arms, never taking his eyes off Howard. "Don't even think about it. There're guns trained on you right this minute. You so much as breathe the wrong fucking way, they'll kill you."

Howard glared at him.

Yeah, it was clear the loan shark was pissed because he'd just been divested of his only leverage.

"What'd I tell you?" Isaiah asked Howard directly.

Howard shrugged.

"I distinctly remember telling you that if you touched one hair on her head, I'd rip your throat out with my bare hands. That sound familiar?"

Cassidy clutched Isaiah's shirt, her hands trembling as she pressed her face against his chest. Unable to resist, Isaiah wrapped his arms around her, holding her tight as he kept his eyes locked with Howard's.

"I wasn't kidding," Isaiah tacked on. "Not one fucking bit."

Cassidy's entire body shook, and Isaiah pressed his lips to the top of her head. "It's okay. You're okay."

He'd told her earlier that they would be taking things one day at a time, but this little stunt had just taken ten years off his life. He hadn't considered what his feelings for her truly meant until Jake had relayed the information that she'd been kidnapped. That had sealed it for him.

Isaiah loved her, and he had no intention of losing her now.

"It's over, baby," he whispered into her ear, hoping to reassure her. "You're safe. You'll always be safe."

She nodded but didn't lift her face.

Jake moved up behind Howard, his weapon drawn while Micah arrived on their other side.

Howard Turner wasn't going anywhere.

"No leverage now," Isaiah told Howard. "But we'd be happy to show you our generous accommodations."

"I want to talk to Max," Howard grunted.

"Unfortunately, Mr. Adorite is otherwise occupied at the moment. However, we expect him to arrive at any time," Isaiah relayed. "You can speak to him in person when he gets here."

As he expected, Howard's eyes widened in fear.

Yes, Max had opted to come to Vegas in order to deal with things himself. His way of making his presence known. The man was one to be respected, and after Howard had so blatantly defied Max, the boss figured it was time to make an appearance.

In an effort to keep the peace, of course.

"Come on," Isaiah whispered to Cassidy. "I'll take you to the penthouse."

"What about the club?" she asked, looking up at him for the first time.

"It's being taken care of."

With his arm around her shoulder, Isaiah steered Cassidy away from the others, leaving Jake and Micah to deal with Howard. They'd put him somewhere safe until Isaiah could deal with him.

"Will I get to meet Max?" Cassidy questioned when they were alone in the elevator.

"Would you like to?" he asked, smiling. Out of all that, the woman chose that tidbit of information to cling to.

"Yeah. I'd like to … thank him."

Isaiah nodded.

"And…" she continued, "I'd like to find out what his plans for Jordan are. I know favors don't come free."

Lifting her chin so that she was looking at him, Isaiah peered into her eyes. "Max didn't do your brother any favors. I did."

Her eyes widened with the news.

"You did? You gave him the money?"

He nodded.

Cassidy patted her bag. "I'll repay you. I've got the cash."

Isaiah shook his head.

The elevator stopped, and he kept his hand on the small of her back, urging her out into the hall. After greeting Frank, Isaiah led her into his penthouse, closing and locking the door behind them.

"Here," she said, thrusting the bag toward him.

"I don't want your money, Cass."

"But…"

"*Jordan* owes me," he said firmly. "And he and I will come to an agreement on how he'll repay the loan. Tomorrow."

"He doesn't have the money," she said quickly, her eyes sad.

"He doesn't need to have it. To pay it off, he'll work for me. In the club."

"But …"

Isaiah placed his hands on her shoulders. "I know he's got a gambling problem. We're going to get him help. You and me. He'll work for me until the loan is paid off and possibly after that." Cupping the side of her face with one hand, Isaiah studied her. "I talked to him, Cass. He knows what he did. He realizes the danger he put you in. And your brother loves you, baby. He's going to get help."

A tear rolled over her smooth cheek, and Isaiah used his thumb to wipe it away.

"Why would you do that for him?"

"I didn't do it for him," Isaiah confessed. "I did it for you."

"Me? Why me?" she inquired.

With both hands, he held her head gently. "Because I love you, Cass."

Her eyes widened in disbelief.

He knew how she felt. He hadn't expected to say those words. Not to anyone. But especially not to a woman he'd met only a day ago.

That didn't make the words any less true.

"One day at a time," he added. "Remember?"

A small smile formed on her lips. "I'm not so sure I like that plan anymore."

Isaiah frowned.

"We don't know what tomorrow will bring," she told him, going up on her toes so that her mouth was closer to his.

"True," he replied, his lips inches from hers. "We don't."

Her smooth fingers caressed his jaw, and he leaned into her palm.

"I love you, too," she whispered. "It's a little unexpected, but…"

"You don't need to explain," he told her. "Just show me. That's all I need."

And with that, Isaiah pressed his lips to hers.

20

LOVE.

That was such a hard emotion to grasp, but as Isaiah held her in his arms, Cassidy knew that was exactly what she was feeling. With his lips pressed to hers so reverently, she could practically imagine the rest of her life with this man.

How that had happened in such a short time, she couldn't understand. Nor would she question it.

At almost thirty years old, Cassidy was beyond trying to figure out how the universe worked. She simply wanted to live her life, enjoy her time there, because as she'd seen in the last twenty-four hours, there was no guarantee on how long they had.

Sliding her tongue along the seam of Isaiah's lips, Cassidy sought more.

He didn't disappoint.

Isaiah's hands slid down her arms, coming around to cup her ass. He lifted her, causing her to wrap her arms around his neck, never breaking the kiss. Pressing her body as close to his as she could, Cassidy held on, moving her tongue along his, inhaling him into her soul.

This man … he'd come into her life by chance, and look where that had gotten them.

Granted, at the moment, it had gotten them into his bed, a place she found she really enjoyed being.

Especially when he was there with her.

It only took a few minutes of groping before they were both naked, skin to skin.

"I want you in my bed every night," Isaiah whispered as he came down over her. "Right here with me."

Cassidy smiled, and it filled her entire being from the tips of her toes to the roots of her hair. Every part of her felt him, the emotion that transpired between them; it was something she'd never felt before. Strong, potent. Invincible.

"Here?" she asked, smiling against his mouth while she ran her hands over every square inch of his perfect body.

"For now," he replied. "At least until we have kids."

Cassidy pulled back to look at him. "Kids?"

"Unless you don't want them."

"No," she said quickly. "I want kids. I just thought…"

"There's plenty about me you don't know yet," he said, kissing her neck. "But you will, Cass. You'll know every part of me the same as I'll know every part of you."

She liked the sound of that. They might still be strangers, but they were tied together by their hearts. As far as she was concerned, that was the first step.

"Kids, huh?" she asked when he stared down at her.

Isaiah nodded.

Cassidy managed to force him onto his back. From there, she crawled over him, her hands gliding over his hard chest, his taut abs. Then down. She found his erection with her fingers, teasing him before wrapping her hand around him.

"There's something else I don't know about you yet," she whispered, grinning up at him.

"What's that?" he asked.

Cassidy leaned down, placing a kiss on the head of his cock before looking back up at him. "Whether or not you like this."

"Oh, I like it. Don't you worry about that," he said on a gruff moan. "Don't stop."

She loved the aggressive side of Isaiah.

Wrapping her lips around the head of his cock, she sucked him into her mouth, using her tongue to lave him, tasting him, inhaling his musky, masculine scent.

"Fuck, Cass. So good."

His hand slid into her hair, holding her head in place while she used her mouth and her hand to pleasure him. He didn't let her stop until he was thrusting his hips upward, driving his cock into her mouth. She took him as deep as she could, using her hand to keep him from going too far.

"Damn, baby. I want to come in your sweet fucking mouth."

A chill raced down her spine; her nipples pebbled from his words alone. She wanted that, too. She wanted to send him over the edge, to make him lose control.

But he had other plans.

"Not yet, though," he growled, releasing her hair and pulling her up so that they were face-to-face.

With ease, he rolled her onto her back, then grabbed a condom from the nightstand. Cassidy watched as he sheathed his thick cock, entranced by the way he gripped himself, stroking slowly. It was so fucking sexy she couldn't look away.

When he was kneeling between her thighs, looking down at her, she finally tore her attention away from his beautiful cock, looking up into his eyes.

"You like that, do you?"

"What?" she asked.

"When I stroke my dick. You like watching me."

Cassidy nodded. Yeah, she liked watching him.

"Good to know."

Her arms went around him when he leaned down to her, her mouth seeking his as he guided his cock into her. Her muscles relaxed enough to take him inside, holding him there, then clenching around the delicious invasion.

"I want this," he breathed against her mouth. "For the rest of my life."

"Me ... too..." Cassidy could hardly breathe for how good it felt. He stretched her completely, the soft hair on his chest tickling her nipples, sending shards of sensation firing beneath her skin.

Isaiah started out slow, but his pace soon increased as he thrust into her, over and over, harder, faster. She clung to him, her eyes closed as she relished the feel of him against her, inside her.

When he growled, Cassidy tightened her inner muscles, locking him to her.

"Fuck, Cass. I'm going to come, baby. Come with me."

Her body caught fire. Rocking with him, she took him deeper, loving the way he felt, the way he smelled, the sound of his voice. It was more than she'd anticipated, more than she thought she deserved.

No, Isaiah Fontenot wasn't perfect, but he was perfect for her. And she loved him.

Without regret.

An animalistic growl tore from his chest as his body stilled, his cock buried deep, and that's when Cassidy let go, her orgasm shattering within her, making her light-headed from the intensity.

Yes, perfect.

21

WITH COURTNEY'S HAND in his, Max Adorite walked into Isaiah's office, briefly scanning the room. His beautiful wife released his hand and went straight for the attractive redhead standing on Isaiah's left.

"Courtney Adorite," she greeted the other woman.

"Cassidy Owens," the redhead replied. "So nice to meet you."

Courtney smiled but then offered the woman a quick hug.

Max watched the interaction, shaking his head. He'd never understand how two women—two complete strangers—could hug one another as though they were long-lost friends.

He then turned his attention to his club manager, who had gotten to his feet as soon as they'd walked in. Isaiah headed toward him, holding out his hand, and Max shook it.

"Things handled?" Max inquired, speaking softly.

"Yes, sir. Our guest is waiting to speak with you. From there, he's got an appointment."

Max knew how to translate, and he appreciated Isaiah's discretion. Then again, the man had always been that way. Very professional, very understanding of the way things worked within his organization. It was the reason Max valued Isaiah, paid him a handsome amount for his loyalty.

"When can I speak with him?" Max inquired.

"Whenever you're ready."

"Courtney," Max said, turning toward his wife. "I need to talk to Isaiah about business. Privately."

His wife nodded, understanding in her gaze. "Cassidy and I will be at the bar."

"After you," Max told Isaiah, allowing the other man to lead him to their *guest.*

"Is Cassidy doing well? After the … altercation." Max had been livid when he'd found out that Howard Turner had dared to come into his hotel and kidnap a woman right out of her hotel room. However, he didn't think his fury had come close to matching Isaiah's. When Isaiah had relayed the information while Max was on the plane, en route, he'd detected the murderous intent in the other man's tone.

He couldn't blame Isaiah. Max would personally end the life of any man who dared put his hands on Courtney. And he'd do it slowly, inflicting as much pain as possible.

So, yes, he understood Isaiah's response.

"How about the brother?"

"I personally settled his debt. I'll be taking him in for the time being."

"You trust him?"

"Not yet, no," Isaiah admitted.

Max also liked that about Isaiah. He was honest.

"But I will. He wants to do right by his sister. I'll be the one to ensure that happens."

Max smiled to himself. He didn't doubt that. "And Micah? How's he doing?"

"Well," Isaiah stated. "He held his own throughout."

"And he's still content?"

When Max had brought the Fontenot twins into his organization, he'd been leery about Micah. The man had a short fuse, despite his fun-loving nature, but from what Max could tell, Isaiah calmed him. The brothers were close, but Max expected now that Isaiah found himself otherwise preoccupied with the pretty redhead, they'd likely need to rely more on Micah to handle things. It was time Micah moved up in the organization, had more responsibility. He was a good man, a loyal employee.

But he would allow Isaiah to handle that. As he did everything that took place at Devil's Playground Las Vegas.

They arrived at their destination, a holding room in the basement of the hotel, a short time later. Max opened the door, stepping into the cold, concrete room.

"Mr. Turner," he said, formally greeting the man, who was currently tied to a chair, completely naked. It was a tactic Max knew well. Most men felt incredibly vulnerable when they were naked. It was an intimidation factor that had worked well for Max over the years. Seemed Isaiah had had the same experience.

"I'm sure Mr. Fontenot has kindly relayed my disappointment," Max said, addressing Howard Turner.

"What the fuck do I care?" Howard retorted.

Max had to hand it to the guy, he was disguising his fear well. Surely the bastard knew he wouldn't be leaving that room alive, yet he still held his own.

"You should've cared," Max said dismissively.

"Why? Because some punk kid thinks he can tell me what to do?"

Max smiled, a feral grin that reflected his hatred for the man.

He did glimpse fear in Howard's eyes at that point.

Moving closer, Max calmly placed his hand around the old bastard's throat, squeezing just enough to cut off his airflow.

"Oh, the pleasure I'd get from killing you."

Howard had the common sense to keep his mouth shut. More than likely, he was trying to conserve oxygen considering Max was allowing him none. Leaning in closer, Max lowered his voice as he said, "Unfortunately, I'm leaving that to Mr. Fontenot. I've learned that you wronged him in a manner that I cannot contend with. He advised me that he'd already made you a promise. I'm of the belief that men should keep their promises."

Releasing Harold's neck, he watched as the man gasped for air.

Turning to Isaiah, he waited for the other man to speak.

"I'd like to allow him to think about what he's done for a while. There's no sense in you wasting your vacation time with this scumbag."

Max agreed. He'd prefer they return to the club, check on the scene. He had no doubt that Isaiah would handle Harold when he was ready. Until then, he agreed that the man would do well with some time to think.

Pivoting on his heel, he faced Harold again. "I'd tell you that, in the future, you should consider respecting others when they request something. However, I don't think that'll matter soon."

With that, he followed Isaiah out of the room, ready to get back to Courtney.

The trek back to the club wasn't as long as before. Or so it seemed.

When they entered the club, Max took it all in. The Fontenot brothers had done well by him for the past five years. They'd taken the club beyond the realm of what Max had anticipated. It continued to thrive, pushing numbers far greater than the Dallas club and remaining on a similar level with the New York club.

"Hey," Courtney greeted when Max joined her at the bar. He kissed her mouth and then glanced over to see Cassidy Owens staring back at them.

"I wanted to thank you, Mr. Adorite," Cassidy said quickly. "I owe you and your wife my life. My brother does, too."

"You owe us nothing," Max told her simply, briefly glancing at Isaiah, who had come to stand beside Cassidy, his arm possessively wrapped over her shoulder.

It was interesting to think that these two had only met a couple of days earlier. Then again, under the circumstances, it made sense that they'd ventured into … whatever this was between them so quickly. Adrenaline tended to make people do things they otherwise might not do. He figured love could potentially be a byproduct of that.

His eyes strayed to Courtney, and he remembered the day he'd met her. He'd been captivated by her, and he'd known at the time that she was different.

He was glad Isaiah had found that as well.

"How about a toast," Courtney said, passing around four shot glasses.

"What are we toasting to?" Max asked.

"To living life," Courtney said, lifting her glass. Max watched as his wife's gaze met Cassidy's.

"Yes, to living life … without regret," Isaiah added.

Max couldn't have said it better himself.

♥▫▫▫▫♥▫▫▫▫♥

I hope you enjoyed Isaiah and Cassidy's story. Without Regret is the first book in the Devil's Playground series, which is a spin-off from the Southern Boy Mafia series. You can read more about Max and Courtney by checking them out on my website.

Want to see some fun stuff related to the Devil's Playground series, you can find extras on my website. Or how about what's coming next? I keep my website updated with the books I'm working on, including the writing progression of what's coming up for the Southern Boy Mafia and the Devil's Playground series.

www.NicoleEdwardsAuthor.com

If you're interested in keeping up to date on the Adorites as well as receiving updates on all that I'm working on, you can sign up for my monthly newsletter.

Want a simple, *fast* way to get updates on new releases? You can also sign up for text messaging on my website. I promise not to spam your phone. This is just my way of letting you know what's happening because I know you're busy, but if you're anything like me, you always have your phone on you.

And last but certainly not least, if you want to see what's going on with me each week, sign up for my weekly Hot Sheet! It's a short, entertaining weekly update of things going on in my life and that of the team that supports me. We're a little crazy at times and this is a firsthand account of our antics.

Keep reading for an excerpt from **Wait for Morning** (Sniper 1 Security, #1) – Available now!

Excerpt from Wait for Morning

One

Connecticut
February

Thump-scrape-thump

Marissa Trexler came awake slowly, trying to fight the groggy feeling as she forced her eyes open. A quick glance at the blurry red digits on the alarm clock told her it was just after midnight. The dim light from the lamp on her bedside table, along with the Kindle resting on her chest, said she'd fallen asleep reading again.

She really needed to stop doing that. More than likely, the suspense novel she'd been engrossed in before she finally dozed off was making her paranoid. Stephen King had a way of doing that to a person.

Sliding the e-reader to the pillow beside her, Marissa scrubbed her eyes with the heels of her hands and glanced over at the bedroom door. Shut and locked. Exactly the way she'd left it. No boogeyman looming over her, ready to do whatever it was that boogeymen did.

She lay there, momentarily listening for the sound that had awoken her. Nothing.

Yep, just as she'd thought. Paranoid. *Thanks a lot, Mr. King.* Maybe it really was time to switch to some lighter reading at night. Perhaps her best friend, Courtney, was right, Marissa should try romance on for size.

Just when she reached for the lamp to shroud the room in darkness so she could attempt to get back to the blessed dreamless state she'd been in, Marissa stopped, her hand hovering inches from the lamp base.

Thump-scrape

Okay, maybe paranoid wasn't the right word because she clearly hadn't imagined the sound *that* time.

Glancing toward her bedroom door once more, Marissa tried to make sense of the noise, but she couldn't. It sounded almost as though someone was dragging something across the floor and then carelessly dropping it. Over and over again.

There was no way that could possibly be it, though.

Right?

Maybe it was the screen door. Yes, that made perfect sense. A much more likely culprit. The damn thing was always coming unlatched, a reoccurring problem with the blistering cold winds slamming brutally against her small rental—aka *safe* house—especially in the dead of winter.

Not for the first time, Marissa wished she was back in Texas. Back where the temperatures weren't freeze-your-nipples-off cold.

Figuring the screen door wouldn't fix itself, Marissa forced her legs over the edge of the bed and slid her feet into her cable-knit boot slippers.

Thump-scrape-thump

A frisson of fear sliced through her at the sound, making her toes curl against the faux fur encasing her feet and causing her heart to slam into her ribs. The screen door was never that consistent.

Swallowing past the lump of ice-cold terror lodged in her suddenly dry throat, Marissa managed to get to her feet. After grabbing her heavy robe from the chair beside the bed, she slowly slipped out of her bedroom, moving down the short, narrow hallway toward the front door as she pulled her robe over trembling arms. Forgoing the lights on her way, she kept her ears tuned to the sound.

Thump-scrape-thump

This time Marissa stopped midstride, standing a mere foot from the doorway that led to the living room as she tried to pinpoint the direction of the noise. It didn't sound like it was coming from the front of the house, which meant … the screen door wasn't the guilty party.

Thump-tha-thump

Thump-tha-thump

Swallowing hard, Marissa realized that new thumping sound was her heart—threatening to beat right out of her chest.

That realization didn't do a damn thing to help the oncoming panic attack.

Thump-scrape-thump

Shit.

Not her heart.

Oh, God!

Marissa listened for a moment, noticing the house was now void of all noise except for the soft rumble of heat through the air vents and the drumbeat coming from her chest. Was the sound coming from behind her? She tried to force her feet to move, but the overwhelming fear kept her rooted in place.

Before the direction to run could make it from her brain to her feet, a hard, firm hand came over her mouth, yanking her back against an equally hard, firm body.

The cobwebs of sleep still saturated her gray matter, making it difficult to register the need to scream, but instinct had her instantly trying to wiggle away.

No! Not again!

A muffled sound escaped her—anything more was hindered by the large palm crushed over her mouth—but it wasn't nearly loud enough to attract help. Or maybe that was the terror lodged in her throat keeping the sound at bay. Either way, she found herself desperately trying to suck in air, stumbling as the massive body behind her pulled her away from the living room, forcing her to shift her feet or fall to the floor.

And yes, she suddenly wondered whether the latter wasn't a bad idea. Getting away should've been her top priority, and Marissa was pretty sure it would've been if she could think clearly.

"Not a word," the deep voice whispered, warm breath brushing against her neck.

Well, that confirmed the answer to the first question that had popped into her head: *man or woman?* Definitely a man.

Low, gruff, familiar, the voice was an oddly soothing rumble against her ear. She recognized the timbre, the cadence, even the inflection, but thanks to the all-consuming dread roiling in the pit of her stomach, she couldn't place it. When she tried to turn, to see who he was, he simply held her flush to his body, continuing to ease them closer to the back door via the darkened kitchen.

"Stay calm. We've gotta get outta here."

His voice was calm, not at all threatening, and the strong arms surrounding her weren't gripping her painfully, but Marissa still questioned: *friend or foe?* She didn't know the right answer, probably because she was still paralyzed with fear.

While her common sense tried to come fully online, the intruder continued to lead her away from the front of the house, and for whatever reason, Marissa found herself complying. Something told her she needed to trust this man.

Less than a minute later, they were stepping outside, the icy winds battering her body, the snow instantly seeping through her slippers, freezing her feet. The blistering cold kick-started her brain, and she glanced at the ski-mask-clad man, who was now reaching for her hand as he rapidly backed away from the house, his intense gaze penetrating her, even though she couldn't even make out the color of his eyes in the inky darkness, darkened even more by the rapidly moving clouds temporarily blocking out the moon.

"Let's go, Marissa!" the man yelled, grabbing her hand and hauling her through the snow that densely covered her backyard.

Was it a good sign that he knew her name?

Okay, so maybe she should've been more worried about the fact that snow was now filling her slippers and saturating her pajama bottoms, or perhaps that she was willingly running *away* from the safety of her house with a man she only thought she should trust.

Unable to form words to argue or even to ask questions, Marissa ran. More accurately, she stumbled through the snow, dredging her way around to the side of the house as fast as she could behind the stranger dressed in black, his clothing of choice a stark contrast against the brilliant white landscape now lit by the moon. Her brain fumbled to make sense of what was going on as her slippered feet trudged through two feet of soft snow blanketing the ground. The gloved hand holding hers felt safe, but for a fraction of a second, she pondered whether she was actually running *toward* disaster rather than running *from* it.

A metallic *ping* sounded from close by, causing her to flinch at the same time her masked companion grabbed her, hauling her close to his solid body and using himself as a human shield, steering her in the direction he apparently wanted her to go.

"In!" the man commanded as they approached a dark SUV haphazardly parked along the side of her house.

Ping.

Ping. Ping.

Holy shit. Was someone *shooting* at them?

With her stupidity level possibly at an all-time high, Marissa didn't question him as he yanked open the driver's door and shoved her into the vehicle, she didn't try to pull away, and she didn't glance back at her house, either, when he yelled, "Other side!" and pushed her across the center console.

"Seat belt!" The brusque word echoed through the chilly interior of the SUV as the engine roared to life when her masked companion hopped in the driver's seat. With frozen fingers, Marissa fumbled with her seat belt while she prayed the heater would push something more than arctic air at her.

How long did it take for frostbite to set in?

Wow. And wasn't *that* an odd question to worry about at a time like this?

Hoping she wasn't going to find out, she forced the notion from her head.

Less than a minute later, Marissa wasn't worried about her numb fingers and toes or even what the sound had been that had woken her in the middle of the night. Her new interest was who this man was and where they were going.

When she turned to face him, ready to pelt him with those exact questions, Marissa was tossed around the front seat like a rag doll—despite the seat belt that was supposed to hold her in place—as he took a turn on what had to be two wheels. Fear gripped her once again as she grabbed for the *oh-shit* handle and held on for dear life. He obviously knew what he was doing, navigating the top-heavy vehicle in polar-like conditions, never taking his eyes off the road.

Chancing another glimpse in his direction, Marissa studied his profile despite the mask still covering his features, trying her best to look at him. *Really* look at him.

When he glanced over at her, tugging the mask off his head, allowing her to see his face for the first time since he'd arrived to whisk her out of the house, her breath lodged in her throat.

What the fuck?

"You're lucky I don't punch you right now," she told him grumpily, earning a chuckle from him.

Continuing to watch him, Marissa willed her heart to stop pounding, her breath to return to normal.

“Since when did they start sending in the big guns?” she muttered when she could breathe again, sarcasm and incredulity replacing the fear that had racked her for the past… According to the blue digits on the dashboard, only fifteen minutes had passed since she’d awoken to the noise.

He didn’t respond.

Before Marissa could blast him for what had happened, there was an explosion that rocked the SUV. Twisting in her seat and peering through the tinted back window, she saw a fireball billowing in the chilly night air.

“Ohmygod… Ohmygod… Oh. My. God.” Marissa turned to eyeball the man who’d come to her rescue. The *last* man she’d expected to see. The *very* man who had just saved her life. “Was that…?”

“Your house? Yeah,” he offered with a slight edge. Although his rich, dark tone reflected a hint of sympathy, his white-gray eyes were hard as steel.

Her house, or rather the residence she’d inhabited for the last two and a half months, was now… *Shit.* It was now a fireball in the sky.

Spinning back around and shifting nervously in her seat, Marissa sucked air into her lungs, praying she wouldn't hyperventilate and pass out. Or maybe that would be better than dealing with this now. Who knew?

A firm hand landed on her back, thrusting her forward.

"Head between your knees, damn it. Don't you dare pass out on me, girl."

Girl? Was he serious right now?

Marissa had no choice but to obey his booming command, as he was simultaneously forcing her head toward the floorboard. Closing her eyes, she slowed her breaths, ignoring the way her hands trembled uncontrollably and her heart raced like a Kentucky Derby racehorse. A few minutes later, when she finally got her bearings, she sat up slowly and asked the one question she felt she'd been asking for far too long. "Who's after me now?"

Once again, no response. *Typical.*

She might never receive an honest answer to that, but at least Marissa had the answer to her earlier question…

Disaster.

Plain and simple.

That was exactly what she'd been running *toward.*

And disaster's name was Trace Kogan.

Acknowledgments

I have to thank my family first, for putting up with my craziness. From my sudden outbursts when I think of something that needs to be added or when I question why one of the characters did what they did, to the strange hours that I keep and the days on end when I'm MIA because I'm under deadline or just engrossed in a story… Y'all are incredibly tolerant of me and for that, I am forever grateful. I love you with all that I am.

My street team – The Naughty & Nice Posse. Ladies, your daily pimping and support fills my heart with so much love. You are a blessing to me, each and every one of you.

My beta readers, Chancy and Denise. Ladies, I'm not sure thanks will ever be enough. However, not only are you the ones who catch the weird things and ask the bigger questions, you've both become my friends and you keep me going.

My copyeditor, Amy. Punctuation and grammar… well, that's not my strong suit. But it is yours and you are truly remarkable at what you do. You simply amaze me and I am so glad that I found you.

Nicole Nation 2.0 for the constant support and love. This group of ladies has kept me going for so long, I'm not sure I'd know what to do without them.

And, of course, YOU, the reader. Your emails, messages, posts, comments, tweets… they mean more to me than you can imagine. I thrive on hearing from you, knowing that my characters and my stories have touched you in some way keeps me going. I've been known to shed a tear or two when reading an email because you simply bring so much joy to my life with your support. I thank you for that.

♥····♥····♥

About Nicole

New York Times and *USA Today* bestselling author Nicole Edwards lives in Austin, Texas with her husband, their three kids, and four rambunctious dogs. When she's not writing about sexy alpha males, Nicole can often be found with her Kindle in hand or making an attempt to keep the dogs happy. You can find her hanging out on Facebook and interacting with her readers - even when she's supposed to be writing.

Nicole also writes contemporary/new adult romance as Timberlyn Scott.

Website
www.NicoleEdwardsAuthor.com

Facebook
www.facebook.com/Author.Nicole.Edwards

Twitter
@NicoleEAuthor

By Nicole Edwards

The Alluring Indulgence Series
Kaleb
Zane
Travis
Holidays with the Walker Brothers
Ethan
Braydon
Sawyer
Brendon

The Austin Arrows Series
Rush
Kaufman

The Bad Boys of Sports Series
Bad Reputation
Bad Business

The Caine Cousins Series
Hard to Hold
Hard to Handle

The Club Destiny Series
Conviction
Temptation
Addicted
Seduction
Infatuation
Captivated
Devotion
Perception
Entrusted
Adored
Distraction

The Coyote Ridge Series
Curtis
Jared

The Dead Heat Ranch Series
Boots Optional
Betting on Grace
Overnight Love

By Nicole Edwards (cont.)

The Devil's Bend Series

Chasing Dreams
Vanishing Dreams

The Devil's Playground Series

Without Regret
Without Restraint

The Office Intrigue Series

Office Intrigue
Intrigued Out of the Office
Their Rebellious Submissive

The Pier 70 Series

Reckless
Fearless
Speechless
Harmless

The Sniper 1 Security Series

Wait for Morning
Never Say Never
Tomorrow's Too Late

The Southern Boy Mafia Series

Beautifully Brutal
Beautifully Loyal

Standalone Novels

A Million Tiny Pieces
Inked on Paper

Writing as Timberlyn Scott

Unhinged
Unraveling
Chaos

Naughty Holiday Editions

2015
2016

BECAUSE NAUGHTY CAN BE OH SO NICE®
NE
LTD

www.ingramcontent.com/pod-product-compliance
Lightning Source LLC
Chambersburg PA
CBHW070326130626
46556CB00007B/2753

* 9 7 8 1 9 3 9 7 8 6 4 7 0 *

Surrender to Peace

by

Rose Allen McCauley

Published by
Olivia Kimbrell Press™

COPYRIGHT NOTICE

Surrender to Peace

PUBLISHED BY: Olivia Kimbrell Press™*, P.O. Box 470, Winchester, KY 40121-0 470. The *Olivia Kimbrell Press*™ colophon and open book logo are trademarks of Olivia Kimbrell Press™. **Olivia Kimbrell Press™ is a publisher offering true to life, meaningful fiction from a Christian worldview intended to uplift the heart and engage the mind.*

Original Cover Art by Amanda Gail Smith (amandagailstudio.com).

Library Cataloging Data

Rose Allen McCauley
Surrender to Peace,/McCauley, Rose Allen
164 p. 20.32cm x 12.7cm (8in x 5in.)

Summary: A broken engagement finds Joy in Puerto Rico with questions for the Lord. Can Benigno earn her love while helping her trust in God once more?

Identifiers: Library of Congress: 2015944145| ISBN-13: 978-1-68190-006-3 (trade) | 978-1-68190-005-6 (POD) | 978-1-68190-004-9 (ebk.)

1. Beach Romance 2. Island Romance 3. Contemporary Romance 4. male and female relationships 5. Christian Inspiration

[PS3568. RM207 A203 2015]
248.8'43 — dc211
